Bumper
Classroom
Clangers

D1395553

Bumper
Classroom
Clangers

A Rowdy Assembly of Howlers and Gaffes

Compiled by
VINCENT SHANLEY

PORTICO

This book is dedicated to all teachers and school personnel, without whose commitment our children and grandchildren would not prosper as they do.

This edition first published in the United Kingdom in 2010 by
Portico Books
10 Southcombe Street
London
W14 0RA

An imprint of Anova Books Company Ltd

ISBN 9781907554124

This edition contains elements of *Classic Classroom Clangers* (2000) and *More Classroom Clangers* (2006) published by Robson Books

A CIP catalogue record for this book is available from the British Library.

10 9 8 7 6 5 4 3

Printed in Great Britain TJ International, Padstow Cornwall

This book can be ordered direct from the publisher at www.anovabooks.com

Contents

Introduction

It is comforting when even the greatest and the famous make gaffes. The difference between them and us more humble folk is that their howlers are captured, more often than not, on video or radio recordings. Most of them, thankfully, have the grace to laugh at themselves and we, for our part, appreciate that "there, but for the grace of God, go I". We laugh not at them, but with them. And so, before we launch into a catalogue of clangers from the world of education, let us enjoy some others from the world of the famous – and sometimes from the not-so-famous . . .

When Ronald Reagan was telling the world that the United States had much to offer the Third World, he made the following error nine times in a speech: "The United States has much to offer the Third World War."

Richard Nixon, attending Charles De Gaulle's funeral: "This is a great day for France."

Entertainer and comedian, Michael Barrymore, compering *Quiz Show:* "So, Carol, you're a housewife and a mother. And have you got any children?"

Jim Siebal, Mayor of St Paul, Minnesota: "I'm not indecisive. Am I indecisive?"

Decca Records executive to the Beatles in 1962: "You'll never make it – four-man groups are out. Go back to Liverpool!"

Samantha Fox, singer/model: "I've got ten pairs of training shoes – one for each day of the week."

In education the gaffes fall thick and fast, and thanks are due to those teachers who have provided such gems as the following, and the hundreds which appear in this book...

Q: Use "judicious" in a sentence.
A: Hands that *do dishes* can be soft as your face, with Mild Green Fairy Liquid.
Q: Who was it who did not like the return of the Prodigal Son?
A: The fatted calf.
Q: What is artificial respiration commonly known as?
A: The kiss of death.
Q: What is the treatment for a badly bleeding nose?
A: Circumcision.
Q: Use "unaware" in a sentence.
A: "Unaware" means your vest and your pants.

So, without further ado, let's read the gaffes from the wise and the not-so- ...

1

Setting the Scene

Mothers, quite literally, find children 'hard to bear' and look forward to the respite bedtime brings. Likewise, most grandparents love their grandchildren to bits but anticipate with glee those soothing words 'bye-bye'. Some people, of course, cannot abide anyone under twenty years of age and would echo the following sentiments.

I abominate the sight of them [children] so much that I have always had the greatest respect for the character of Herod. *(Lord Byron)*

I think children shouldn't be seen or heard. *(Jo Brand)*

Alligators have the right idea. They eat their young. *(Eve Arden)*

I love children, especially when they cry, for then someone takes them away. *(Nancy Mitford)*

W.C. Fields suggested to a friend who was having trouble with his daughter that he should 'throw her overboard'. When he received the response: 'You can't throw your own daughter overboard,' he replied, 'Why not? Let the sharks protect themselves.'

Those who are parents accept that there will be trials and tribulations on the path to adulthood (or 'adultery' as one young lad mistakenly called it) and know that those who protest along the lines of 'our children never caused us a moment's worry', are telling lies. Some are realistic or, perhaps, more cynical.

Money – the one thing that keeps us in touch with our children. *(Gyles Brandreth)*

I've got two wonderful children – and two out of five isn't bad. *(Henry Youngman)*

We all, of course, are aware that children can be rascals and challenging, and for that reason we can sympathise and empathise with the following situations and observations.

This is Miss Hambridge, our new schoolteacher. She's between nervous breakdowns. *(The Moon's Our Home)*

Noel Coward once attended a dreary play written around a fourteen-year-old so-called 'prodigy', who was on stage for most of the piece. 'Two things should have been cut,' Coward remarked. 'The second act and that youngster's throat.'

'Once when I was lost, I saw a policeman and asked him to help me find my parents,' Rodney Dangerfield recalled. 'I said, "Do you think we'll ever find them?" He said, "I don't know, kid. There are so many places they can hide."'

Never raise your hands to your kids – you leave your groin unprotected. *(Anon)*

Be nice to your kids – they will choose your nursing home. *(Anon)*

Having one child makes you a parent; having two makes you a referee. *(David Frost)*

However, love them or loathe them, one of their greatest attractions is the mirth and merriment they create with their 'bloopers' or 'gaffes'. We laugh not at them, but with them, because these 'clangers' are the result of their innocence, enthusiasm and their striving to learn and perfect their mother tongue. Very often they bring a level-headedness and realism to a situation hitherto unperceived. There is an abundance of common sense in the following answers.

Teacher: What was the first thing your mother said to you this morning?

Pupil: She said, 'where am I, Cathy?'

Teacher: And why did that upset you?

Pupil: Because my name is Susan, Miss.

Teacher: ALL your responses MUST be oral, OK? Which school did you go to?

Pupil: Oral.

Teacher: What is your date of birth?

Pupil: 18 July

Teacher: What year?

Pupil: Every year, Miss.

Perchance the following mistakes could well be the fault of grown-ups' lack of clear enunciation.

Q: Name one book written by Thomas Hardy.
A: Tess of the Dormobiles.

'Dour' means a kind of help like in the hymn, 'O God Dour Helping Ages Past'.

Then we have the replies that are almost there; they have come within a whisker of making it.

Granny says alcohol will be the urination of my uncle Bobby.

I believe muggers, whether they are men or women, should be put behind bras.

But it is not, of course, only children who drop 'clangers'. All of us, whether we be high and mighty, rich or poor, famous or insignificant, powerful or feeble, have our moments of madness or bouts of pure ignorance when we perpetrate gaffes. Such television programmes as It'll Be All Right On The Night would seem to suggest that committing 'clangers' is in vogue and de rigueur. The sensible stance to take, something actors seem to have realised, is that we accept our lack of perfection and have the good grace and humility to laugh with others.

While much of the following material concentrates on pupils, let us not forget that head teachers can come out with statements that cause staff and pupils to hoot with hilarity – when they are not there, of course.

Whenever I open my mouth, some fool speaks. *(Said at assembly)*

In two words – impossible.

My deputy head has been depressed since he began working with me in 2001.

Parents themselves send in letters of excuse or explanation that are sometimes humorous and beyond belief.

Thomas couldn't do his homework last night because we had to worm the dog.

I am pleased to tell you that my husband, who was reported missing, is dead.

Please excuse my daughter for being late. Her broom wouldn't start so I had to send it back to Salem for repairs!

However, it cannot be denied that the more influential, self-satisfied, superior and conceited a person is, the more we enjoy them making a cock-up. George W. Bush obtained little sympathy when he declared: 'I have opinions of my own – strong opinions – but I don't always agree with them'; or former vice-President Dan Quayle, when he expressed the view: 'I was recently on a tour of Latin America, and the only regret I have was that I didn't study Latin harder at school so I could converse with those people.' Perhaps George W. inherited his problems of communication from his father, Bush Senior, who must have scared the wits out of his presidential challenger by announcing: 'I'll put my manhood up against his any time.'

Unfortunately for those in the public eye, their gaffes are likely to be recorded and shared, whereas we lesser mortals have only our friends or family to chortle with pleasure and satisfaction.

This year's hairstyle is called a 'shag' and our resident styl-ist is here to give our model one. *(Lorraine Kelly)*

Born in Italy, most of his fights have been in his native New York. *(Des Lynam)*

MINERS REFUSE TO WORK AFTER DEATH. *(Headline in Economic Review)*

Such gaffes from the media abound and, in recognition of this, the final sections of this book are dedicated to them. Meanwhile, it's the children's turn.

2

The Curriculum

We all have our memories of favourite subjects at school which usually spring from an empathy we had with a kindly teacher or a facility for a subject which, by the grace of God, was naturally bestowed upon us. That is not to say that our proficiency in that discipline protects us against dropping clangers.

Who can forget the report on TV of a certain American senator, promoting "Spelling Week" in a school, who displayed his skills at the blackboard by putting an "e" at the end of potato?

Yes, even the best of us can slip up, and the more important and self-opinionated the person dropping the clanger, the more enjoyable it is for those who witness it.

Certain subjects are more popular than others. English, history and geography, for example, figure largely, mainly because pupils can always write something and rarely reach an impasse – unlike maths or a Greek translation, in which a dead end as final as the summit of Everest can rapidly be reached.

Still, it must brighten up the day of the marginalised

classics teacher when this type of letter appears in a national newspaper . . .

As a normal wife and mother, I have found Latin immensely helpful in every way. *(Letter in Daily Mail)*

Careers / Work Experience

When it comes to a choice of career, there are those who have no doubt in their minds about what they want to do, especially after sampling certain jobs through "work experience", which one pupil described as "the start of adultery life".

After attending James Hawes Funeral Parlour for his "work experience", school leaver Trevor Newman, 16, said: "I participated in a cremation, visited a mortuary, and was shown a body. It was great. What's more, if they take me on, I'll never be out of a job." *(Waltham Forest Guardian)*

I want to be a butcher because I like meating people.

Q: List the careers you are considering.
A: I want to be a pote.

I would like to be a braim surgian.

Punctuation can make all the difference . . .

Student desires post; domesticated, fond of cooking children.

Extracts from work experience application forms handed in . . .

Wish: To end all the killing in the world.
Hobbies: Hunting and fishing.

Q: Are you a natural born British subject?
A: No – by Cæsarian section.
Q: Length of residence in Britain *(if applicable)*
A: 26 ft.

One school leaver was applying for a brickwork course. Under the title "Examinations to date" were four columns. "Subject", "Grade" and "Date" were neatly completed for his five exam passes. But under the fourth heading, "Board", was written: "Yes I was", "lots", "not so much", "no" and "yes, very much".

Others know what they want to do but don't get the chance . . .

Arriving at Messrs Trimmings of Castleford to start her first day's work, Miss Alison Knaggs, who has been unemployed since leaving school two years ago, was told that she was redundant. "I did not have time to take off my coat," she said, "but a spokesman for the firm said he understood how I felt."

Man, honest. Will take anything.

Some get no sympathy . . .

Delia Morrison has been barred from her parents' home because she married a grave-digger. Her mother, 55-year-old Mrs Gladys Peat, of Geneva Drive, Darlington, Co. Durham, said yesterday: "We have never felt so ashamed in our lives. If we had known what he was we would have thrown him out long ago." *(Sunday Express)*

... while others get all the sympathy ...

Henry, aged 20, whose godparents include the Duchess of Gloucester and the Duke of Kent, is a jazz drummer who went to Eton. "But he's been on the dole lately," said Bunty. "Which is a bit sad when he's so close to the Queen." *(News of the World)*

Some are in no doubt as to what should happen or should not ...

Mrs Dimmock deplored the fact that young people no longer went into private service. She thought that, apart from the pleasant relationship that existed between employer and employee, the servant picked up a far better accent. *(Worthing Gazette)*

"Do you gents want something to drink?", though said in a perfectly friendly manner, was not, in my view, the right way for a wine waiter to address First Class passengers. *(Sunday Times)*

Others have no idea what is happening ...

A 19-year-old girl told a Canterbury court today that she was getting married on Saturday but did not know her fiancé's job. Asked by the clerk for her fiancé's occupation, she replied: "I have never asked him. I know he goes out each day." *(Evening Standard)*

But there are plenty of good careers on offer – aren't there?

DENIS HEALEY COMMUNITY CENTRE: Foundry Mill Street, Seacroft, Leeds 14. PART-TIME CLEANER – £24,551 per hour. *(Leeds City Council Dept of Education)*

DO YOU SCRATCH your bottom while taking a bath? Have it re-glazed by the professional. *(Edinburgh Advertiser)*

Tired of cleaning yourself? Let me do it.

FOLDERS FOR SALE: Stock up and save. Limit: one.

PURLER Tornado would train girl to ride wall of death; good knitter preferable. *(Southend Standard)*

SINGLE GIRL GROOM REQUIRED TO WORK UNDER STUD GROOM. Able to ride/exercise.

URGENTLY WANTED BY MACHINE TOOL FACTORY. Male parts handlers. Box 132.

WANTED 50 girls for stripping machine operators in factory.

WANTED Unmarried girls to pick fresh fruit and produce at night.

And others not so good . . .

WANTED . . . EDIBLE OIL TECHNOLOGIST *(The Observer)*

HELP WANTED Man wanted to handle dynamite. Must be able to travel unexpectedly. *(Daily News, Newfoundland)*

```
URGENTLY REQUIRED — Pump Attendant
PART-TIME — 126 hrs week
Apply: Whittlesey Motors Ltd
EASTREA ROAD, WHITTLESEY,
PETERBOROUGH
```

(Peterborough Evening Telegraph)

WANTED Smart Young Man for butcher's. Able to cut, skewer and serve a customer. *(Local paper)*

Woman wants cleaning three days a week. *(Guardian)*

WANTED Chambermaid in rectory. Love in, £475 a month.

MORTGAGE RESEARCHERS Required for prestigious offices in Hamilton Square. To work with small friendly professional team. Flexible shits 5 pm-9 pm. Excellent hourly rate, plus bonuses. Due to expansion, immediate positions. *(London Advertiser)*

TOILET CLEANER required 5-8 pm, Mon-Fri in Kew, Richmond. Good rates of pay. Must be able to ride a bicycle. Please call Hazel Nish on . . . *(Hatford Tribune)*

ENGINEERING
SETTING OUT ENGINEER — SELF EMPLOYMENT
HIGH WYCOMBE   £11,000 PER HOUR

(Hertfordshire's "Job Opportunities")

YOGA INSTRUCTOR
PERMANENT POSITION
You must have minimum level 3 standard combined with excellent customer service skills and the ability to work unsupervised.

(Sheffield Star)

WANTED IMMEDIATELY A woman for boiling down. Apply Blake Potted Meat Company *(New Zealand newspaper)*

WANTED Women, Evening Shift, 5.30 to 9.30, for backwashing, regilling, and tophat minding. *(Bradford Telegraph and Argus)*

Unexpected vacancy for a knife-thrower's assistant. Rehearsals start immediately. Apply in writing to Black Horse Lodge, Linford, Milton Keynes. *(Bedfordshire Times)*

The Royal Navy is sometimes called the senile service.

To help new graduates into the world of work, a New York research firm asked personnel executives at 200 leading companies to describe the worst gaffes they had witnessed in the interview room. Here are some of the replies . . .

One candidate arranged for a pizza to be delivered to my office during the lunch-hour interview I had arranged with him. I asked him not to eat it until later.

When I mentioned that we had gone to the same school, he immediately stood up and began to belt out the school anthem.

On the phone I asked the candidate to bring his CV and a couple of references. He arrived with his CV and two people.'

When I asked the candidate to give a good example of the organisational skills she was boasting about, she said she was proud of her ability to pack her suitcase "real neat" for her vacations.

I once had a candidate who actually showed up for an interview during the summer wearing a bathing suit. She said she didn't think I'd mind.

One candidate couldn't answer any of my questions because he had just had major dental work.

English

A class had been asked to write an essay on "The funniest thing I ever saw". The lazy boy of the class sat dreaming away while the other boys were busy writing. Soon his teacher went up to his desk to see his effort. It ran as follows: "The funniest thing I ever saw was too funny for words."

Essay "on a ceremony you have witnessed": "When the wedding was over the bridegroom clasped his loved one tight in his arms, while the little organ began to swell and fill the room."

Transparent is something you can see through – like a keyhole.

Q: What is a young horse called?
A: A clot.

I met Miss Enid Blyton, whose books for children have sold 40,000,000 copies, and asked her how she works. "Some writers plan chapters and work things out in advance," she said. "I just sit down and open the sluice gates and it just pours through." *(Daily Express)*

We do feel that an improvement with her English language would help her if she is to persue a career in banking. *(Work experience report)*

On day three of the term, September 1998, after the "Literacy Hour" had been introduced into primary schools, a ten-year-old enthusiastically enquired: "Sir, when are we going to do that 'leprosy hour'?"

How can the French expect to attract our tourist trade? This year, at five different French hotels, the tap marked *"C"* turned out to be *"H"*. *(Letter in Evening Chronicle)*

I really felt sacred as I waited for the dentist.

Rusty, a pony owned by a 16-year-old grammar school girl, Elizabeth Millbank, of East Street, Blandford, Dorset, is terrified by fireworks. So, on 5 November, she will sit with him and read Shakespeare aloud. *(Daily Mail)*

Barbarians are little metal balls you put in wheels to make them run smoothly.

"What is 'wanderlust'?" was a question put to senior girls at a Southend school. One girl replied: "It is what people go on cruises for."

Dear Mrs — J. has not learnt the lines for English as I don't think he needs to learn about Shackespear. Something else would of been better. I should think they want to learn

proper English first. *(Letter from a parent to a Dorset teacher)*

Q: Name one book written by Thomas Hardy.
A: Tess of the Dormobiles.

A census is where everybody in the house has to be filled in.

The judge said that he had been living off the immortal earnings of his wife.

The answer to the following question makes it clear that the little lad knew that the word "frugal" had something to do with saving . . .

Q: Show that you know the exact meaning of "frugal" by writing a short paragraph including the word.
A: A beautiful princess was at the top of a tall tower. She saw a handsome prince riding by. "Frugal me, frugal me," cried the beautiful princess. So the handsome prince climbed the tall tower and he frugalled her and they lived happily ever after.

Last night it was so cold when I got in from school, I switched on the emotion heater and had a hot bath.

To scotch something means to drown your sorrows in whisky.

The little lad asked the school for a copy of *She Stoops to Conga*.

Q: Use the word "foul" in a sentence.
A: My dad took all the family to Birtsmorton Water Foul Sanctuary on Sunday.

A buttress is the wife of a butler.

Q: What is the plural of potato?
A: Turnip.

A deaf mute is a dead dog.

Q: Give the opposite of "filly".
A: Empty.

Hogmanay is another type of wood.

A rudder is what you milk a cow with.

Never look a gift horse in the ear.

Heroine is a hard drug which is addictive.

Q: Who was Robinson Crusoe?
A: A famous singer.

Q: What is a brassière?
A: Something you warm your hands on.

Q: What's a suspended sentence?
A: Where the man gets hanged.

Q: Write a word which describes a man who keeps on despite all difficulties?
A: Passionate.

The girl insisted on riding side-salad.

Another tragic thing in our family was my brother.

The boys earned some money by cleaning widows.

Schools without capital punishment are rather boring. Without capital punishment nobody pays any attention.

On *The Highwayman*: They gagged Bess and tied her to a narrow bed. From this we know that she was a virgin because she still had a narrow bed.

On *Dulce Et Decorum Est*: You can imagine the misery he must have felt, being alive one day and dead the next.

Excerpt from *Lady Macbeth's Diary*: "Macbeth will kill him tonight. It's a shame really; he struck me as a nice man."

Shakespeare wrote tragedies, comedies and hysterectomies, all in Islamic petameter.

Most of Shakespeare's plays are terrible tragedies.

An example of a heroic couplet are Romeo and Juliet.

Romeo's wish was to be laid by Juliet.

Miguel Cervantes wrote *Donkey Hote*.

John Milton wrote *Paradise Lost*. Then his wife died and he wrote *Paradise Regained*.

Q: How did Odysseus trick the Cyclops?
A: He told him that his name was Norman.

McAnulty's Yellow Line
Coach Tours and Private Hire
"Les Miserable"
Point Theatre, Dublin
Limited Number of Tickets available

(Newry Reporter)

As I approached the house, I saw a man mowing the lawn with a small child.

My family condescended from Wealdstone.

There was the pupil who thought Shakespeare came from Arabia.

Her father was a civil serpent.

As he walked through the room he heard the sound of heavy breeding.

The heroine has to be like Julius Caesar's wife – all things to all men.

Complete the following: "A stitch in time . . ."
". . . is worth it because you don't have to buy a new jumper."

Complete the following: "A rolling stone gathers . . ."
". . . a fair bit of speed."

The vicar was wearing his cossack.

My dad has an infinity with birds.

It seems the man was a blank clerk.

I put my foot on a sharp tack which made my foot howl with pain.

Q: Explain the circumstances in which this quote from Macbeth was made: "I heard the owls scream and the crickets cry."
A: Macbeth was on his way to murder Duncan when he heard the call of nature.

Teacher: Josh [six-year-old] – What do you do when you come to a full stop?
Josh: Er . . . You get off, Miss.

Q: What form of verse best describes 'Mary Had A Little Lamb' and 'Little Jack Horner'?
A: Mercenary rhymes.

A goblet is a male turkey.

Q: Use the word "tackle" in a sentence.
A: A tack'll make you sore if you sit on it.

All sentences are either simple or confound.

Rhythm is a horse trotting on a road.

The Royal Wedding was a whore inspiring event.

He spent his days in prison sewing children's balls together.

The octopus wrapped his testicles round the diver and strangled him.

Correctly English in 100 Days – East Asian book title.

If you ever come within a mile of our house, will you stop there all night?

Q: Use the word "denial" in a sentence.
A: Cleopatra lived on Denial.

For his comfort the roadman has a brassière which is very nice on a cold day.

Horoscopes
Due to unforeseen circumstances we are unable to bring you horoscopes this edition!

(The Journal of Yarm & District)

A 1982 circular from the Joint Matriculation Board Examinations Council announced ...

It has been decided to modify the format of the English Literature (Advanced) Paper I. In future, in order to avoid

any possibility of confusion, section B will consist of essay questions on the plays of Shakespaere.

A teacher from a school in the south of England told the story of the occasion when a colleague in the English Department invited an eminent French poet to give a talk to his second-year class. For 40 minutes the guest gave an interesting discourse. At the end, he offered to answer pupils' questions. There was a pause before one young boy plucked up the courage. "Sir," he asked respectfully. "How much did your trainers cost?"

Q: Name a famous "Willy".
A: Willy the Poo.

Q: Give the opposite of woe.
A: Giddyup.

. . . they were married and lived happily even after.

(Malvern Gazette and Ledbury Reporter)

WANTED Man to take care of cow that does not smoke or drink. *(Herald)*

WANTED A domesticated lady to live with an elderly lady to hell with cooking and housework. *(Agency magazine)*

Work for the Lord. The pay isn't good, but the retirement benefits are out of this World. *(Church bulletin board)*.

Monotony means being married to the same person all of your life.

And what of English around the world . . .?
I've said goodbye to boyhood – now I'm looking forward to

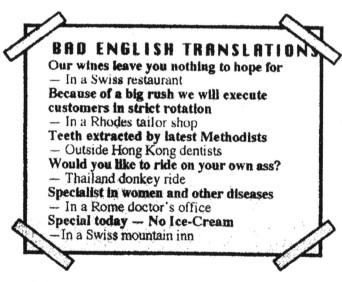

BAD ENGLISH TRANSLATIONS

Our wines leave you nothing to hope for
— In a Swiss restaurant
Because of a big rush we will execute customers in strict rotation
— In a Rhodes tailor shop
Teeth extracted by latest Methodists
— Outside Hong Kong dentists
Would you like to ride on your own ass?
— Thailand donkey ride
Specialist in women and other diseases
— In a Rome doctor's office
Special today — No Ice-Cream
— In a Swiss mountain inn

my adultery.

Still, even the greatest can make mistakes . . .

Jane Austen from *Northanger Abbey*: Such was Catherine Morland at ten. At fifteen appearances were mending; she began to cut her hair and long for balls.

Man jailed after restaurant row

Indian staff terrified as he demands italian food

(Evening Express)

Charles Dickens from *Little Dorrit:* No public business of any kind could possibly be done at any time, without the acquiescence of the Circumlocution Office. Its finger was in the largest public pie, and in the smallest public tart.

From *The Last of the Valerii:* Next after that slow-coming, slow-going smile of her lover, it was the rusty complexion of his patrimonial marbles that she most prized.

Russell Ash and Brian Lake have located some unusual British titles in their Bizarre Books *(Pavilion)* . . .

Peculiar Pastimes

Teach Yourself Alcoholism, by Glatt Meier (EUP, 1975)

How to Pick Pockets: A Treatise on the Fundamental Principle, Theory and Practice of Picking Pockets, by Eddie Joseph (Vampire Press, 1946)

The Great Pantyhose Crafts Book, by Ed & Stevie Baldwin (Western Publishing Co., 1962)

Build Your Own Hindenberg, by Alan Rose (Putnam, 1983)

Hand Grenade Throwing as a College Sport, by Lewis Omer (Spalding & Bros, 1918)

Books to Make the Heart Sink

The Romance of Cement, by the Portland Cement Company (Liverpool & Knight, 1926)

I Was a Kamikaze, by Ryuji Nagatsuke (Aberlard-Schuman, 1973)

The Wit of Prince Philip, by HRH Prince Philip (Leslie Frewin, 1953)

The Sunny Side of Bereavement, by Rev. Charles E. Cooledge (Gorham Press)

Premature Burial and How It May Be Prevented, by William Tebb & Edward Perry Vollum (Sonneschein, 1986)

Do-It-Yourself Coffins: For Pets and People, by Dale Power (Schiffer, 1997)

Specialised Subjects

Truncheons: Their Romance and Reality, by Erland Fenn Clark (Herbert Jenkins, 1935)

American Bottom Archaeology, by Charles John Bareis & James Warren Porter (University of Illinois Press, 1983)

Whippings and Lashings, by The Girl Guide Association (1977)

Inappropriate Authors

Oh! Sex Education, by Mary Breasted (Praeger, 1970)

Motorcycling For Beginners, by Geoff Carless (EP Publishing 1980)

Death in Early America, by Margaret Coffin (E P Dutton, New York, 1976)

Vasectomy: Male Sterilising, by Paul J. Gillette (Paperback Library, New York, 1972)

Medicine

The Complete Guide to Selling Your Organs, Body Fluids, Bodily Functions, and Being a Human Guinea Pig, by Jim Hogshire (Loompanics, 1992)

The Romance of Leprosy, by E. Mackerchar (Lepers Mission, 1949)

What You Didn't Know About France

A local food speciality of Provence is a quack monsieur.

Small cafés in France are good for eating snakes.

We saw a girl in our hotel with frogs' legs.

Many Frenchmen wear berries on their heads.

French children drink bowels of hot chocolate.

In France, school is compulsive from the age of six.

At Chateaudun, if you want to go for a long walk, you can walk along the river Loire.

Fish are soled in Brittany.

A past President of France was called Guillotine.

On French motorways they have toll-boobs.

Fruits de mer are fruits of the sea, eg coconuts and pineapples.

Fruits de mer are cockles and wenches.

The French have a two hour dinner break because they find it more fascinating than us.

When driving in France, it is very easy to get confused – so don't forget to drive on the left.

In France the whine is much cheaper.

At the citadel in Boulogne, we saw the spot where the Unknown Worrier rested.

Prices are high on the Eiffel Tower.

If crossing the Channel by car, you have to book a fairy.

Grapes are pressed and they excrete their juice.

Beaujolais Nouveau is a health food.

Cabernet d'Anjou and Saumur are French political parties.

The Arc de Triomphe is famous for the forbidden soldier who is buried on top of the arch.

At the Arc de Triomphe, you can see the infernal flame.

The Arc de Triomphe is the biggest horse race in France.

I had a sandwich and a white café au lait.

You get information from the French Tourist Bored.

We visited Notre Dam.

Quasimodo made the bell at Notre Dame.

La mère works in the town hall.

The religious event which takes place when a French boy or girl reaches the age of 13 is: circumcision or castration.

Parasites are the inhabitants of Paris.

Literal translations . . .
Est-il parti, ma tante? Is there a party, my aunt?

Sacré Coeur. Holy Dog.

La raison du plus fort est toujours la meilleure. The biggest raisins are always the best.

La pauvre femme tourna vers . . . The poor woman turned green . . .

Un grand garçon à lunettes. A big lunatic boy.

J'ai grand faim. I have a big wife.

Beurre. Cold.

Pas de deux. Father of twins.

Coup de grace. Lawn mower.

Avez-vous des timbres? Have you any wood?

Je voudrais une fiche. I would like a cod.

Est-ce qu'il y a un bon bistro ici, s'il vous plaît? Could you pass the gravy here, please?

La brasserie est grande et bonne. The brassière is large but good.

Je voudrais prendre pour mon petit déjeuner un oeuf a la coque dur. I would like to have for my breakfast a hard cock's egg.

Voulez-vous poisson hors-d'oeuvre? Do you want fish or duvre?

Le chef vous propose. The chef would like to marry you.

Je voudrais une bouteille de vin rouge. I would like a bottle of rough wine.

Je voudrais louer une bicyclette. I need a bike to get to the toilet.

Sommes-nous bien sur la route pour Paris? Do we pass the Somme on the way to Paris?

General Knowledge

Give an example of the following . . .

An occupation where you need a torch.
A: A burglar.

A dangerous race.
A: The Vikings.

Some famous brothers.
A: Bonnie and Clyde.

A part of the body beginning with "N".
A: Knee.

Something you put on walls.
A: Roofs.

Something that floats in the bath.
A: Water.

A famous Royal.
A: Mail.

Something in the garden which is green.
A: The shed.

Something slippery.
A: A conman.

A food that can be brown or white.
A: Potatoes.

A famous Scotsman.
A: Jock.

Something you do in the bathroom.
A: Decorate.

A song with "moon" in the title.
A: Blue Suede Moon.

A famous bridge.
A: Bridge Over Troubled Water.

A bird with a long neck.
A: Naomi Campbell.

Something you open other than a door.
A: Your bowels.

When the court is assembled the judges come out of the robbing-room.

Q: What is the currency used in Denmark?
A: The Denmark.

Remembrance Day is on a Sunday, for the First and Second World Wars. Thousands of popsies are sold in the streets.

The Royal Prerogative is the little dog the Queen goes around with.

Q: What do the letters HRH stand for?
A: Duke of Edinburgh.

Q: How does the law define "actual bodily harm"?
A: It means actually harming someone's body.

Q: What should you do if you get obscene telephone calls?
A: Ask the operator to stop them.

Q: Name a paint which protects wood.
A: Brown.

Q: How do prescription drugs vary from over-the-counter drugs?
A: Some drugs have a more lusting effect.

Q: Why are some farmers in favour of fox hunting?
A: Because it gives them the chance of dressing up.

Q: Who would you expect to see with a mortar board?
A: A bricklayer's mate who has to keep the bricklayer in bricks.

Q: What is anthropology the study of?
A: Ants.

People have to pass MOT tests every 12000 miles.

Q: What do the letters "MW" mean on a radio?
A: It must not be used on top of a microwave.

Q: What is an exporter?
A: Somebody who used to have a job carrying cases at railway stations.

Q: What do you get from the pine tree?
A: Pineapples.

Q: What are steroids?
A: Things for keeping the carpet on the stairs.

Pupil: Miss, what's Huntingdon's Chorea?
Teacher: It's a hereditary disease which is quite common in isolated communities where they're so interbred.
Pupil: Do they have a lot of bread shops there, then, Miss?

If you have no money, you could try the porn brokers.

Q: Why does a surgeon wear a mask when he performs an operation?
A: So if he messes it up the patient won't know who did it.

Aristotle Onassis was a Greek shitting typoon.

Slogan by pupil devising an anti-smoking poster . . .

GIVE UP SMOKING – NO BUTTS

Geography

European errors . . .

The steamer sailed from Dieppe to Newheaven.

Q: Which is the nearest port to Dover?
A: Calais – unless you go by aeroplane.

The advantage of living on an island is that you get the spray from the sea.

Q: Name a Spanish holiday resort.
A: El Dorado

Nobody goes to Lloret de Mar anymore. It's too crowded.

Today, Rome is full of fallen arches.

The Mediterranean and the Red Sea are connected by the sewage canal.

Q: What is the capital of Spain?
A: "S".

Lancashire and Cheshire exam question: "On the outline map of England and Wales provided, shade in the Highlands of Scotland."

American absurdities . . .

Q: How are buildings in San Francisco built to be safe from earthquakes?
A: The buildings don't quite touch the ground.

Some parts of the Grand Canyon are a mile deep and two miles high.

Difficulties facing the American farmers of the Mid-West are draughts and incests.

General geographical gaffes . . .

Q: What is the major export of Brazil?
A: Brazil nuts – but only at Christmas.

To make rubber you cut the bark off a hyena tree. The rubber is then smoked.

The climate of the Sahara is such that the inhabitants have

to live elsewhere.

Q: What is the correct name for the method of providing water for crops in dry areas?
A: Irritation.

Tea-bushes sometimes grow to 20 feet tall, but as the women are only five feet, they have their tops cut off.

Q: Write down what you know of Red China.
A: It looks nice on a white tablecloth.

The cold at the North Pole is so great that the towns are not inhabited there.

An Eskimo lives on a kind of leather called blubber.

Q: What are "glaciers"?
A: People who fix windows when they're broken.

Q: What is the Equator?
A: It is a menagerie lion running around the Earth through Africa.

GREENLAND VOLCANO IN ERUPTION by arrangement with *The Times (The Scotsman)*

Q: Name the five continents.
A: a, e, i, o, u.

British blunders . . .

Cooler in the South, warmer in the South is the seven-day forecast of the *Sunday Express* weather experts. *(Sunday Express)*

Sheffield is in a valley in Yorkshire slopping up the side of the moorland.

Q: What is the best way to protect crops from storms?
A: By planting trees. A 60ft tree can break wind from 300 yards.

Q: Name a cow that gives a lot of milk.
A: Daisy.

Q: Give an area of low population density.
A: Graveyard.

Manchester is one of the densest cities.

During the strikes under Margaret Thatcher, the coal industry was nearly destroyed when the miners were driven into the ground.

Crewe is the biggest conjunction in England.

The Zulus lived in mud huts and used to have rough mating on the floors.

And parents will do even more than can be expected to give their offspring a place in life . . .

Seeking to improve her young son's poor knowledge of geography, a Norfolk reader persuaded him to take up stamp collecting. Only two weeks later, she had striking proof of how wise she had been. "Where is Spain?" she asked him. Without hesitation he replied: "Five pages after Portugal."

(Overheard) I cannot believe it. That geography project has

to be handed in tomorrow. I feel really sorry for Mam – it'll take her ages.

History

Ancient, and not so ancient, history . . .

The world began millions of years ago with little orgasms crawling around it.

Ancient Egypt was inhabited by Mummies who wrote in hydraulics.

The Egyptians built the pyramids in the shape of a huge rectangular cube.

The Greeks were lazy people because they worshipped idles.

The Greeks were highly sculptured people.

The Greeks had myths. A myth is a female moth.

Socrates died of an overdose of wedlock.

In the Olympic games, the reward to the victor was a coral wreath.

Q: What is the name given in Greek mythology to the creature that was half man and half animal?
A: Buffalo Bill.

The government of Athens was democratic because the people took the law into their own hands.

The Punic Wars were fought between the Romans and the Carthage Indians.

1st pupil: What's Carthage, anyway?
2nd pupil: You know – it's that stuff in your bones.
3rd pupil: Don't be silly – that's carnage.

Sparta protested, saying that all the cities' fornications in Greece should be dismantled.

Julius Caesar extinguished himself on the battlefields of Gaul.

Brutus stabbed Caesar. Dying, he gasped out: "Tee, hee, Brutus."

At Roman banquets the Romans wore garlics in their hair.

The Romans were called Romans because they never stayed in one place for very long.

The artichoke was an ancient instrument of torture.

Because of the good roads in Rome, Christianity travelled faster than ever before.

King Arthur lived in the age of shivery with brave knights on prancing horses and beautiful women.

King Harold mustarded his troops before the Battle of Hastings.

Year 8 were watching a video on the Norman Conquest and the commentator referred to William the Conqueror, adding "also known as William the Bastard". One of the lads asked the teacher: "Sir, what's a bastard?"

"A bastard," said the stoical teacher, "is when a child is born to a couple who are not married."

Another little lad, as proud as Punch, announced to the class: "Hey, Sir, I'm one of them, then."

Magna Carta provided that no free man could be hanged twice for the same offence.

In midevil times most people were alliterate.

During this time, people put on morality plays about ghosts, goblins, virgins and other mythical creatures.

Q: What does "impregnable" mean?
A: It means that you cannot have babies.

William Tell invented the telephone.

William Tell shot an arrow through an apple while standing on his son's head.

Martin Luther was a German pheasant.

Martin Luther was excommunicated by a bull and nailed to the door at Wittenburg Cathedral.

Protestants disliked the smell of incest in the Catholic Church.

It was Donatello's interest in the female nude which made him the father of the Renaissance.

Q: What was Leonardo da Vinci's major claim to fame?
A: Sailing the *Mona Lisa* round the world.

Christopher Columbus was a great navigator who discovered America while cursing about the Atlantic.

Columbus' ships were called the *Nina*, the *Pinta* and the *Santa Fe*.

Henry VIII always had difficulty getting Catherine of Aragon pregnant.

Some of Henry VIII's wives were – Chattering of Aragon, Amber Lin, Jane Saymore, Ann of Cloves and Catherine Purr.

From the womb of Henry VIII protestantism was born.

Q: What stood Henry VIII apart from all other English Kings?
A: He was the fattest human being of all time.

Queen Elizabeth was the "Virgin Queen". When she exposed herself before her troops, they all cheered.

And Sir Francis Drake said: "Let the *Armada* wait. My bowels cannot."

Queen Elizabeth knitted Sir Walter Raleigh a cardigan.

Mary, Queen of Scots, married the Dolphin of France.

Children were born every year in the 18th century.

Q: Explain the importance of Wat Tyler.
A: Wat Tyler is a magazine for bathroom fixture handymen.

America was discovered by Colombo.

Later, the Pilgrims crossed the ocean, and this was called the Pilgrim's Progress. The winter of 1620 was a hard one for the settlers. Many people died and many babies were born. Captain John Smith was responsible for all this.

American Indians used to live, and some still do, in a reservoir.

Q: What were the three major causes of the American Civil War?
A: (a) Indians, (b) Hot weather, (c) Arguing.

Finally the American colonists won the war and no longer had to pay for taxis.

Benjamin Franklin died in 1790 and is still dead.

Abraham Lincoln was born in a log cabin that he built with his own hands.

On the night of 14 April 1865, Lincoln went to the theatre and got shot in his seat.

Under the constitution of the United States the people enjoyed the right to bare arms.

The watchwords of the French Revolution were Liberty, Equality, Maternity.

All through the French Revolution the women of France knitted and they dropped a stitch every time a head fell into the gelatine.

Napoleon wanted an heir to inherit his power but since Josephine was a baroness, she couldn't have any children.

Jacques Cartier, while searching for the North West Passage, stumbled across the great St Lawrence River and mapped it.

Queen Victoria was the longest Queen.

Queen Victoria sat on the thorn for 63 years.

Queen Victoria was a moral woman who practised virtue. Her death was the final event which ended her reign.

Wellington's nickname was "Ironpants".

Q: Name two of the key figures in the Industrial Revolution. *A:* Margaret Thatcher and Arthur Scargill.

In the nineteenth century, people stopped reproducing by hand and started reproducing by machine.

Cyrus McCormick invented the McCormick raper, which did the work of a hundred men.

The invention of the steamboat caused a network of rivers to spring up.

Florence Nightingale was a woman from a very early age.

Victorian ladies had thrills around their bottoms.

Charles Darwin was a naturalist who wrote *The Organ of the Species.*

Karl Marx became one of the Marx Brothers.

The First World War ushered in a new era in the anals of human history.

Universal suffrage was when the whole world suffered.

Q: With what do you connect the name Baden-Powell?
A: You connect it with a hyphen.

When Vesuvius erupted, there were floods of molten lager flowing down the mountainside.

Q: Name a great man of this century.
A: Martian Luther King.

Anne Frank hid in an attic for two years so the Romans couldn't get her.

The Russian Revolution was an uprising from the bottom.

Another important invention was the circulation of the blood.

Q: Describe what life was like in the trenches during the First World War.
A: It was OK when soldiers sang songs like "Anyone Who Had A Heart" to keep their spirits up.

When the soldiers went to battle in 1914 they had no idea what they were letting themselves in for. They thought it would be just like they saw on the telly with the British always beating the Germans and like the cowboys always beating the Indians.
The year 1936 was fairly uneventful. George V died and Edward VIII abdicated. The Crystal Palace burned down. Benny Goodman launched the swing era. The prophesied end of the world proved less nigh than anticipated. But perhaps the event with the greatest long-term significance was the staging of the first Hotel and Catering Exhibition at Olympia. *(Natural Gas magazine)*

Hitler was a madman, and this was his fatal floor.

Asked "What was the wartime Black Market?" in an Eden Camp History Theme Museum questionnaire, one pupil wrote: "For most people, the Black Market meant a little fiddle with the woman who owned the corner shop."

One way to settle the Middle East problem would be for the Jews and Arabs to sit down together and settle this like good Christians.

Q: What is Britain's highest award for valour in war?
A: Nelson's Column.

Home Economics

It has never been the same since they stopped cooking at school . . .

Q: Name a chicken dish with spices.
A: Chicken in Harpic.

Q: Chow mein is a popular Chinese dish. Name some others.
A: Kebabs and also chips with curry sauce.

Q: For how long would you boil a size 3 egg?
A: For no longer than four hours.

And how you do it throws up some novel methods . . .

My old uncle has an unusual pulse beat – sixty to the minute. Without the help of a clock, he can time accurately eggs boiling for three minutes, rounds of boxing and the two minutes' silence on Armistice Day. *(Letter in Illustrated)*

And . . .

Sir, The hymn "Onward Christian Soldiers", sung to the right tune and in a not-too-brisk tempo, makes a very good egg timer. If you put the egg into boiling water and sing all five verses and the chorus, the egg will be just right when you come to "Amen". *(Letter in the Daily Telegraph, 1983)*

Q: How would you keep milk from going sour?
A: Leave it in the cow.

A vegetarian is a horse doctor.

Then add the milk and the butter and rub the mixture well into the floor. *(Cookery book)*

Due to copy error, we regret that the Surprise Apple Sweet Potato recipe in the October issue was incomplete. Please add: 4 cups of mashed potatoes and 3 large apples. *(Cannery publication)*

At the end of the school's two hour itinerary, refreshments were provided by Ready-Mix Concrete Ltd. *(Eastwood and Kimberley Advertiser)*

Keeping all food under cover is the first step towards ridding the house of aunts.

To prevent tears when peeling onions, either bite on a slice of bread or work under a running tap and breathe through the mouth.

An oyster is a fish built like a nut.

A gripe is a ripe grape.

School's Daily Specials include select offerings of beef, foul, fresh vegetables, salads, quiche.

A number of stories have emerged about certain star footballers' lack of culinary awareness . . .

One reporter, who refused to divulge the name of the England international concerned, recounted sitting next to him at the Professional Footballers' Awards. The waitress asked him whether he would care for the "fish hors d'oeuvre". He replied: "You had better give me the d'oeuvre – the fish plays havoc with my stomach."

On another occasion, a footballer asked for "café au lait, please – and would you make it white".

And can it be true that one, when asked if he would like a prawn cocktail, replied: "No thanks, I'll have a drink with my main meal."

. . . and, asked whether he liked scampi, responded:

"Yeah, I love all Walt Disney's films."

One story, which is true, at least according to ex-international, Chris Waddle, concerns his friend Gazza. Apparently, on a pre-season tour of New Zealand, when the two were colleagues at Newcastle, Gazza came down late for breakfast at the team's hotel. "What can I get you?" asked the waitress. "I'll have a full English breakfast," replied Gazza. "I'm sorry," said the waitress, "but I'm afraid we've run out of bacon." "What?" exclaimed Gazza. "40 million sheep and no bacon?"

When the late and great Matt Busby joined the Forces during the Second World War, the recruiting sergeant asked him his occupation. "Footballer," replied Matt in his strong Scottish accent. When he was posted to his new unit, he found out that he had been registered as a "food boiler".

West Ham and England striker Ian Wright when asked during one of his first TV interviewing slots, "What's your favourite 'haute cuisine'?", responded, "Hot food."

But back to food . . .

Q: Give an example of unacceptable food hygiene.
A: If you find a bird dropping on a table – it's not all right to eat it.

Q: What rights do you have if you are sold out-of-date food?
A: You have the right to see the manager and bring it up in his office.

Q: If a person is feeling ill, why is it not a good idea for them to be serving food.

A: Because it is dangerous for deceased people to carry hot food.

Miss, you know it says on the work-sheet that I have to clean the cooker inside and out? Well, I've tried, but it is too heavy for me to get it into the playground.

If you want to be a cookery teacher you must spend a lot of time cooking yourself.

Q: What is rhubarb?
A: A kind of celery gone bloodshot.

Husk fresh corn; spread ears lightly with peanut butter. Place on grill, turning until done – about 10 minutes. Or let everyone grill his own ears, using long skewers to do so.

Marinade the steak in the sauce for at least two hours, then cook under a hot grill, basting with the sauce at frequent intervals. Alternatively, pour off sauce after marinading, heat separately, and let your guests pour it over themselves.

This packet of ready-made pastry will make enough for four persons or twelve tarts.

And other aspects of home economics . . .

Miss, I can't find the invisible thread.

Q: What's a bidet?
A: It's a thing that keeps you warm in bed.

Freelance eggs are more natural than battery-produced ones.

When buying cutting-out shears, consider – "Do they succumb to my needs?"

The mail order protection scheme is not being able to try underwear on because it is unhygienic.

Diets are for those who are thick and tired of it.

Now that preservatives have been introduced, the life expectancy of food is much longer.

If teeth are not cleaned, plague is the result.

And babies . . .

To avoid accidents always keep your hair in a net and never have a baby in the kitchen.

Q: How can parents help when a child wakes in the night suffering from breathing difficulties?
A: Make them inhale a steam kettle.

Q: What is the purpose of a placenta?
A: It's a place where you leave children when you do your shopping.

The first thing the doctor has to do when the baby is born is he has to cut the biblical cord.

If the baby does not thrive on fresh milk then it should be boiled.

When my Mam had the baby, she told my Dad to phone for the ambulance when the contraptions were 10 minutes apart.

Pregnant women get sudden urges for things like pomigranits.

And sorry . . . wrong order:

RETRACTION The "Greek Special" is a huge 18 inch pizza and not a huge 18 inch penis, as described in an ad. Blondie's Pizza would like to apologize for any confusion Friday's ad may have caused. *(Daily Californian)*

Maths

Sky reporter speaking with a young supporter outside Elland Road before a Leeds United v Manchester United League match:

Reporter: Who's going to win tonight, then?
Little lad: Leeds.
Reporter: And who's going to score?
Little lad: Lee Sharpe.
Reporter: How long have you supported Leeds, then?
Little lad: (Pause) Er . . . six years.
Reporter: And how old are you?
Little lad: Four.

Q: Does anyone know what a ratio is?
A: Please, Miss, I think he's a sailor.

Q: If a single ticket costs £26.48, how much does a return ticket cost?
A: Twice as much as that.

Q: How would you share 20p between four men?
A: I wouldn't because it's hardly worth it.

Q: If six boys and five girls want to go to the farm for their outing, how many would that be altogether?
A: All of them, Miss.

When one class was asked to draw two lines of symmetry, one pupil drew two lines of gravestones.

A circle is a round straight line with a hole in the middle.

A Year 6 Maths SAT test posed the question: If one can of Coke and a bag of popcorn costs £1.45 and the Coke cost 90p, how much does the popcorn cost? Give reasons for your answer.
A: 60p – because that is what my Mam pays when she goes to the pictures on a Saturday night.

Teacher: Right, Tommy. A mother has five children and only four potatoes to share among them. If she wanted to give each child an equal share, how would she do it?
Tommy: Mash them, Miss.

If you asked six friends to name the commonest bird in Britain, the odds are that nine out of ten would say the sparrow. *(Weekend)*

I have been informed that the school bus companies will be getting 12 new drivers – 5 men and 4 women. *(Parent's newsletter)*

30,000 pigeons were released, filling the air with the flutter of a million wings.

Music

The following commentary was heard and recorded from a BBC *Music and Movement* programme for children: "We are going to play a hiding and finding game. Now, are your balls high up or are they low down? Close your eyes a minute and dance around, and look for them. Are they high up? Or are they low down? If you have found your balls, toss them over your shoulder and play with them."

While on the subject of innocence . . .

The little girl had just visited a local comprehensive school to watch a musical play. "Which school was it?" asked her mother. "Oh, it was that Catholic school – the Immaculate Contraption."

Mrs Nightingale of Swallow Street has reopened her music school. Phone Robin for appointment. *(Eastern Province Herald)*

What is it about string musicians which cause problems . . . ?

Nero was a cruel tyrant who would torture his poor subjects by playing the fiddle to them.

He clearly fitted into the same category as the following musician . . .

"What do you think of the violinist?" George Bernard Shaw was once asked by one of his students.
"He reminds me of Paderewski," replied Shaw.
"But Paderewski is not a violinist."
"And neither is this gentleman."

The Old Malthouse School has just produced a short history which includes some memories at random, such as that of the music master who said his favourite instrument was the viola because so few boys played it. *(The Old Malthouse Mag)*

The new automatic couplings fitted to the organ at Hyde public school will enable Mr R*** to change his combinations without moving his feet. *(Hyde Old Boys' Magazine)*

A tangerine is one of the smallest members of the percussion family.

A folk-singer is someone who sings through his nose by ear.

The music teacher stopped the orchestra for the umpteenth time and addressed the drummer: "George, I don't expect you to be with us all the time, but I would greatly appreciate it if you would be good enough to keep in touch now and again."

The story is told that, as a courageous but not gifted boy called Rodney sang "Danny Boy" at the Christmas school panto, a lady in the audience began to cry uncontrollably. "Are you Irish?" asked the usher. "No," replied the lady. "I'm his singing teacher."

The western side play Country and Western, the Scottish play the Gay Gordons. Where would we be without music?

Beethoven wrote music even though he was deaf. He was so deaf he wrote loud music.

Mozart was a child orgy.

Mozart lived until the end of his life.

Her singing was mutiny on the High Cs.

Wagner wrote music which is better than it sounds.

Ten musicians from the Western Orchestral Society – incorporating the Bournemouth Sympathy Orchestra and Bournemouth Sinfonietta – are to lose their jobs. *(Daily Telegraph)*

Beethoven was a great composer. He wrote many works. He also had a large family and used to practise on the spinster upstairs.

Q: For what was Stradivarius famous?
A: For discovering the upper layer of the atmosphere.

Q: Why is one of the composer Handel's best known works

called "The Water Music"?
A: Because he lived on an island.

Sign on Music Department entrance – **Bach After Lunch**.

An orchestra has a man called a conductor who stands out in front with a piece of paper which tells him what music the orchestra is playing.

But as we all know, conductors are too clever and perceptive merely to do that – or are they?

On his first day in charge, the story is told of the new conductor addressing the orchestra: "From now on, things are going to be different around here. Everyone will be expected to be on time and work long hours."
   Displeased with this, the tympanist beat on the drums: "BOOM, BOOM-BOOM BOOM."
   "All right," said the conductor. "Who did that?"

The 150 members of the Queensland Flute Guild were asked not to wear backless dresses at the Brisbane Conservatorium of Music concert. "Please wear high-back dresses," pleaded their president, James Carson. Asked why, he said: "We want to pin sheet music on their backs. They can come frontless, but not backless." *(Sheffield Star)*

"LEONORE" – ONLY OPERA BEETHOVEN WROTE ON MONDAY EVENING *(San Antonio Express, Texas)*

Peter Henly, the winner of the Cassel Silver Medal for the best boy musician in the school, will play a corset solo during the concert. *(East Kent Mercury)*

A CORRECTION: In a caption in last night's *Evening*

Gazette, Dorothy Duffney, conductor of the Cleveland Musical Society, was described as Mrs Vera Beadle. She is, of course, Mrs K. Atkinson, of Hartburn Lane, Stockton. *(Evening Gazette)*

Nature Study

In winter bullfinches are best fed on bacon rinds and great tits like coconuts.

A kangaroo keeps its baby in its porch.

A cuckoo is a bird which lays other birds' eggs in its own nest and viva voce.

Australia's animals include the kangaroo and the Coca-Cola bear.

Fish swim about in shawls.

An Australian dog is called a dingy.

In cold weather Eskimos turn their skins inside out to trap the heat.

The camel is the sheep of the desert.

A lion is a tiger with black and white dots.

Q: What is the essential difference between an annual and a bi-annual plant?
A: An annual is the name given to a plant which dies every year. Bi-annuals only die once.

Q: What is a Kiwi?

A: A type of polish.

Q: What would you find in an orchard?
A: Flowers.

Q: What's the obvious advantage of camels holding lots of water?
A: They rarely go to the toilet.

And some unusual questions . . .

What do unicorns eat?

Do camels have to be licensed in India?

Is it legal to keep an octopus in a private house?

A quorum is a place to keep fish in.

An artist specialising in marine paintings of storms at sea had some of his work exhibited at St Ives. A schoolgirl who studied the paintings and was then introduced to the artist exclaimed with deep sympathy: "You really do have terrible luck with the weather."

Q: What has four legs and flies?
A: A dead horse.

Q: How might it be possible to stop a nosebleed?
A: Put the nose much lower than the body until the heart stops.

Q: What should you do if a dog bites you?
A: Put the dog away for several days. If it has not recovered, then kill it.

I think some dogs ought to be compulsorily castrated. They should not be allowed to increase willy-nilly.

Religious Education

The Old Testament can cause some confusion . . .

The first book of the Bible is Guinessis.

The first pair ate the first apple.

Cain, one of the sons of Adam and Eve, asked: "Am I my brother's son?"

In the Old Testament, but not in the New, it's an I for an I."

Teacher to eight-year-old: "George, what name did God give the first man?"
George: "Adam, Miss."
Teacher: "And the first lady?"
George: "Did he call her Madam, Miss?"

Noah built an ark, which the animals come on to in pears.

Goliath was a bit bigger than a telephone box.

The last book in the Bible is the Epilogue.

"Moses was found floating on the River Trent."

Moses went up on Mount Cyanide to get the Ten Commandments. He died before he ever reached Canada.

Moses came down from Mount Sinai with the tabloids.

Moses led the Hebrew slaves to the Red Sea, where they made unleavened bread which is bread without any ingredients.

Solomon, one of David's sons, had 300 wives and 700 porcupines.

Jacob, son of Isaac, stole his brother's birthmark.

One of Jacob's sons, Joseph, gave refuse to the Israelites.

The Jews were a proud people and throughout history they had trouble with the unsympathetic Genitals.

As can the New Testament . . .

Jesus was born in Bethlehem, at the age of 32, I think.

Jesus was caught preying.

Jesus walked along the road to Jerusalem with his 12 decibels.

Jesus was erased from the dead.

The Jews were disappointed with Jesus because He was not that kinder leader.

. . . and it turned out to be the Good Smartin.

Q: What were Jesus' final words to the Apostles at the Last Supper?
A: Who's going to do the washing up then?

The kingdom of God is wherever you would like it to be. It has no bounders.

The Sunday School teacher asked a little girl if she knew who Matthew was. The answer was no. The teacher then asked if she knew who John was. Again the answer was no. Finally the teacher asked if she knew who Peter was. She answered: "I think he was a rabbit."

Q: Was it lawful to buy or sell on the Sabbath Day?
A: Buy.

And a general idea of religious practices and beliefs . . .

Almost every church in England had an authorised virgin tied to the pulpit.

We are always getting the Geneva Witnesses knocking on our door.

On Whit Sunday all the disciples had a touch of wind in the Upper Room.

St Patrick chased all the bad snacks out of Ireland.

Q: Who is the patron saint of travellers?
A: St Pancras.

Humidity is the distinctively Christian virtue.

The epistles were the wives of the apostles.

Jesus was born by supernatural contraception.

Jesus healed people with very bad illnesses, like the Widow of Nairn's son – he was so ill he was dead.

Q: What was the name of the saint who looked after all the birds and the animals?
A: It was Francis of Onassis.

Our Lady and all the angels have lilos on their heads.

Last weekend, the Bishop came to our school and turned some of the Sisters into Mothers in a short, but very interesting, ceremony.

The Pope, at this time, was inflammable.

The little Scottish girl was asked what was the safest way of crossing the road. Her answer: "By the presbyterian crossing."

Q: Give an example of a "white lie".
A: My library book was overdue once and I said that I couldn't get down there through the flue.

Q: Describe two of the projects CAFOD supports in the Third World. Explain how they help to serve those suffering from poverty.
A: CAFOD supports places like Bosnia. They try and give people food. Also in places like Euthanasia people are dying every day.

Q: Complete the following: 'Those who live by the sword . . .
A: . . . will get shot by those who don't.

From a 1998 GCSE Religious Education examination paper: Suffering may raise a problem for religious believers, but thanks to the ingenuity of the Bible, most things can be explained – and when they can't, RE teachers may make something up.

Q: Many people are reluctant to share what they have. Suggest reasons for this.
A: Because some people are greedy and want everything.

People like this should be shot.

Some people think of heaven as all fluffy clouds and no sex.

Although I'm a Methodist, and therefore not a Christian, I believe in God.

People who do wrong are always paid out by God, but I wish he'd hurry up about it.

A seven-year-old insisted on telling his teacher what he thought the Commandment "Thou shalt not commit adultery" meant. "Miss, it means that you shouldn't put water with the milk."

Q: Name two hymns to the Blessed Virgin.
A: 1. Hail Holy Queen 2. Mary Had A Little Lamb

A young gentile pupil visiting a Jewish school asked one of the sixth-formers if the glasses he was wearing were special ones that you needed to read Hebrew.

Sister Eulalia was sitting meditating at her window when she saw, from her first-floor room, an obviously dejected and depressed "gentleman of the road" sitting on the convent wall with his head in his hands. Taking pity on him, she folded £5 into a note with the words "Don't Despair – Sister Eulalia" written on it. She then threw it towards him where it landed at his feet.

The next day, Sister Eulalia was told that a man was at the door, insisting on seeing her. She found the stranger of yesterday waiting. Without a word he handed her some money. "What's this?" she asked. "It's your £50. Don't Despair came in at 10 to 1."

Irreligion is one of the great faiths of the world.

Monks sleep in dormitories and sometimes lay brothers.

Evening Subject: "What is Hell like?" Come and hear our new organ. *(St James's Boarding School's Sunday Service)*

NOTE: In some of our copies the article "The Power of the Papacy" described the Pope as "His Satanic Majesty"; this should read "the Roman Antichrist". *(Protestant Telegraph)*

Science

A twelve-year-old girl's school essay on "The Opposite Sex" is reported to have included the sentence: "I do not think much of the opposite sex because when I want to do anything they want to do the opposite."

Conversation was about the flight of the American space shuttle and the four-year-old daughter, who had been listening in, was asked if she knew what space was. "Yes," she replied immediately, "a place in the car park."

The light passes into the eye through the lens and is focused on the rectum.

Germans are so small that there may be as many as one billion, seven hundred million of them in a drop of water.

Nitrogen is not found in Ireland because it is not found in a free state.

One of the wonders of modern science is bringing a dead body back to life through artificial insemination.

Water is composed of two gins, oxygin and hydrogin.

Blood flows down one leg and up the other.

Germinate: To become a naturalised German.

Vacuum: A large empty space where the Pope lives.

Gravity was invented by Isaac Walton. It is chiefly noticeable in Autumn when apples are falling off the trees.

Comotose is when you get dead feet, like when you get frostbite.

Q: What is the difference between lightning and electricity?

A: We do not have to pay for lightning.

Q: What safety advice would you give to somebody working with acids and reactive materials?
A: BE CAREFUL!

Heli Bop comet has been visible at night to the naked since January.

Pure water must contain hydrogen because oxygen would float away if it was not for hydrogen.

Q: What is Charles Darwin best known for?
A: His book – *The Origin of the Speeches.*

Q: Why do you think it is important for houses to have windows?
A: It gives you a chance to see burglars before they can get in.

Q: What changes happen to your body as you age?
A: When you get old, so do your bowels and you can get intercontinental.

The blood flows through the alimentary canal into the abdominal canopy.

The cow has a pulse as well as anybody else.

Q: What is an animal with a backbone called?
A: A vibrator.
And . . .

TARANTULA – When a scientist dies in agony with his head swollen to twice its normal size and his hand grown claw-like, only Matt, the young town doctor, is suspicious.
(Review in Lincolnshire Free Press)

3

Overheard – In the Playground and Elsewhere

Well, why don't you like lads wiv 'airy ear'oles then?

1st girl: Jimmy walked me home from the shops last night. I don't like him much.
2nd girl: Neither do I – he's only after one thing.
1st girl: Yes, I know, he's always cadging yer fags.

1st girl: I've just been to *Evita*.
2nd girl: You don't look very brown.

1st boy: Did you have a good holiday in Spain?
2nd boy: Yeah – it was great.
1st boy: Was the flight OK?
2nd boy: Yeah – but I was glad to get back on terracotta.

I wonder how much deeper the ocean would be without sponges?

Honk if you love peace and quiet.

Small boy: Daddy, why are we going here? *Father:* To get away from your mother.

Woman to small boy: Take your cap off, Patrick, so that the wind can blow the dandruff from your hair.

Dad to son on beach: Now tell Daddy where you buried the keys.

Boy: You're not normal.
Girl: Yes I am. I've always been normal.
Boy: No, you're not. As long as I've known you, you've never been normal.
Girl: Yes I am. My mam and dad are normal too – it's our Joanne who has to use shampoo for greasy hair.

1st girl: I have a set of silk undies. They're lovely, but they cost a lot.
2nd girl: I have a silk nightie.
1st girl: That's nice. I could never afford anything like that.
2nd girl: I didn't buy it. My sister gave it to me. She bought it for her honeymoon and never wore it.

Overheard in grocery store . . .

Patron: Are they twins?
Wife: Yes.
Patron: Are they both yours?

Two young teenagers were discussing the time, in the future, when they might get married. "I'm not having any of this woman's lib stuff," the lad declared firmly. "I'm going to be the boss and you'll do as I say." Then he added: "Would that be all right with you?"

"Mary, where is Utopia?"
"I'm not sure, but I think it's in the Mediterranean."

1st little girl: The angel said Mary was going to have a baby and she had one the next day.
2nd little girl: Don't be silly – it takes a year.

Little girl: Is it true that when you die you go to Devon?

1st girl: I have to go to the hospital to visit my granny tonight.
2nd girl: What's the matter with her?
1st girl: I'm not sure really, but my mam says it's a serious operation – something about a hysterical rectum.

Q: How can he remember all that?
A: He's got a pornographic memory.

And you have no idea how difficult it is, actually, to get a budgerigar out of a treacle tart.

One boy to another: "I had one up my trouser leg last year."

I don't like the play, but I've got the best bit. I have to say: "Bubble, bubble, toilet trouble."

1st student: You would get bored watching Olivier play Hamlet.
2nd student: Well, I don't like football – especially foreign teams.

Overheard in Rimini: "Hey, Mam, they've even got pizzas in Italy."

A mother and small son were walking past the statue of David in Rome and the mother was saying to him: "No, George, you should know – Big Ben is a clock."

Two lads having an argument in the playground – one said to the other: "Hey, don't fly off at a tangerine."

On a bus passing a cinema . . .

First girl: I don't fancy that, do you?
Second girl: What's that then?
First girl: Going to see that Richard the 'undreth and eleventh.

1st boy: We went to Bamburgh Sands on Saturday.
2nd boy: Was it nice?
1st boy: Well, there's miles and miles of sand. Did you know they filmed part of *Lawrence of Olivier* there?

I wish I could have had her legs – on her they're such a waste.

If I had a figure like 'ers, I'd walk on me hands.

I wish my backside was as flat as his.

We went to Blenheim Palace. The grounds were lovely and were designed by Capability Smith.

It was a Catholic school's governors' meeting where the new parish priest had not met fellow-governors, one of whom was a nun in charge of the convent. The chairman introduced them thus: "Father, you haven't met Mother, have you?"

Overheard at a football match: "Come on, Our Lady of the Most Holy Rosary, get stuck in."

Pupil welcoming guests: "Can I take your clothes off?"

Overheard in playground: "Well, her dad's the head-teacher, she's bound to get RIP treatment."

1st boy: Hey, Sean, what's that on your cheek?
2nd boy: It's a birthmark.
1st boy: Really. How long have you had it?

In restaurant . . .

Mother to waiter: Could I take what my son has not eaten, which is most of his dinner, home for the dog?
Three-year-old: We don't have a dog, Mammy.

Girl: My mam had to go to see about her bad back yesterday.
Teacher: Is it any better?
Girl: Yes, a lot. She said the psychopath was very good.

My granny is in hospital for an operation on a detached retinue.

What he lacks in intelligence, he makes up for in stupidity.

He is very clever but sometimes he lets his brains go to his head.

Why did your mam name the baby John? Every Tom, Dick and Harry is called John.

"Our George is going to court today."
"Why – what's he done?"
"Nothing, he's been called as a witness for the prostitution."

A girl, explaining why her father, a philosophy PhD, can't give medical advice: "He's a doctor, but not the kind that does anyone any good."

In a restaurant where there was a kids' ball pool (an area filled with plastic balls), a little girl ran up to her father and exclaimed: "Daddy, I've just kissed Jason in the balls."

An elder sister talking to her little brother going into church:
Sister: They won't allow you to talk, you know.
Little brother: Who won't?
Sister: The Hushers.

Teacher: The hike will be over ten miles long.
Little lad: Does that mean we'll need long walking socks, Miss?

Then there's always the comic . . .

Father to little boy of five or six: "If you don't stop whining, Margaret Thatcher will come and get you."

At the zoo where some small boys were looking up at a giraffe: "Bloomin' heck, hasn't he got a long way to wee."

Overheard in classroom: "My dad's the second best fighter in the town – whenever he has a fight he always comes second."

One man confiding to another: "When it came to education, my father wanted me to have all the opportunities he never had. He sent me to a girls' school."

1st teacher: How is it that you know so much about plants?
2nd teacher: Well, when my husband died, I buried myself in the garden.

As a child I had every toy my father wanted.

And where do they get them from?

First little boy: I like goldfish.
Second little boy: So do I, but when you're swimming among them, they suck yer arms.

"I've got a very soft spot for our headteacher," said the obviously irate young lady. "A swamp."

I'm really mad – that really has got my dandruff up.

1st boy: When I was in Spain, I nearly got stung by one of those huge jellyfish.
2nd boy: You mean the Portuguese menopause?

Just look at your fingers. They're filthy. Suck them – go on – suck them.

Her mam used to take her to the school bus every morning and meet her off it again at night. She still doesn't know how she got pregnant.

The scene is the top of a bus where a little girl is sucking a lolly and now and again rubbing it on the fur coat of the lady in front of her. Her mother said: "Don't do that, you'll get hairs all over your lolly."

The class of seven-year-olds were learning the difference between "sh-" and "ch-", aided by pictures of ships and churches. One perceptive little girl politely pointed out: "Please, Miss – this rule doesn't work all the time, does it?" "Yes it does, Charlotte," insisted her teacher.

"Do you enjoy Kipling?"
"Don't know – never been kippled."

4

Children

Children are not everyone's favourite people. It could be that some are resented because they are too clever by half than the adults with whom they associate. Parents who feel this way will enjoy the definition of a precocious child as one who took his nose apart to see what made it run. In fact, some parents show a positive aversion to them even when they care for them themselves.

Prince Philip, himself a father of four, said in October that the population problem could be solved if unwanted children were not born. And, he claimed, most children after the second were not wanted. *(Sun)*

Most of us parents know that, in order to keep down the price of school lunches, meat in some dishes is being partly or wholly replaced by protein made from soya beans. But what about the Cambridgeshire school which is offering its pupils fried codpieces? *(New Public Service)*

I've often wondered what little brothers were for. *(John McEnroe after beating Patrick)*

I don't play with my children. I can't tolerate whingers. *(Chris Eubank on family life)*

You wouldn't believe it, but the same kids who are eating you out of house and home are never there. *(Hal Roache)*

Insanity is hereditary. You get it from your kids. *(Graffiti, London, 1979)*

My mother loved children – she would have given anything if I'd been one. *(Groucho Marx)*

I think I was popular with my teachers . . . on Saturdays and Sundays. *(Eric Morecambe)*

BOYS ASSORTED SIZES £20

(Isle of Wight County Press)

He didn't like children. He finished his drink with a silent toast to Herod. *(Kingsley Amis)*

One in four children are the result of undersired pregnancies. *(Scanorama magazine)*

The more I see of children, the more I like dogs.

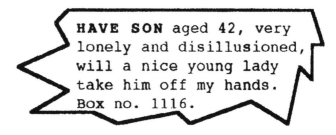

```
HAVE SON aged 42, very
lonely and disillusioned,
will a nice young lady
take him off my hands.
Box no. 1116.
```

(Wellington Star, Taunton)

The kidnappers took me to Jersey, bound and gagged, and my parents finally realised that I'd been kidnapped and they snapped into action . . . They rented out my room. *(Woody Allen)*

Ah, the patter of little feet around the house. There's nothing like having a midget for a butler. *(W. C. Fields)*

I love children . . . parboiled. *(W. C. Fields)*

Boys will be boys – and so will a lot of middle-aged men.

Of course children brighten up a home. They never turn the lights off.

MENU
Fish and Chips – £3.50; 1 Piece Fish – £2.70
Chips & Peas – £1.50; Children – £1.00
(Bridlington Restaurant)

A 12-year-old boy was shot dead by a sentry on duty outside a fort in Lisbon. The sentry reported that the boy ignored his challenge in the dark. Army officials last night carried out a reconstruction of the events. A civilian, Carlos Chaves, aged 33, played the role of the boy. He too was shot dead. *(Newcastle Evening Chronicle)*

A doctor has compiled a list of poisons which children may drink at home. *(Ottawa Journal)*

Whether you like them or not, there can be no argument that sometimes children can come out with comments and views which add to the brightness of the day. They can show a remarkable innocence and a commonsense view of situations which can evade and reduce to guffaws and hilarity the most hardened critics and observers of life.

In church for the first time, the little boy watched, wide-eyed, as the choir, all in white surplices, filed in. With wonder in his voice he whispered: "Are all those people going to get their hair cut?"

Teacher Gillian Freeman tells the following story . . .

On playground duty, I was approached by a pair of outraged five-year-olds who told me that their friend Stephen was eating worms. I hotfooted it over to the suspect, who was standing suspiciously close to the flower bed.

"Stephen, are you eating worms?" I demanded.

"No, Mrs Freeman," he replied indignantly.

I was greatly relieved, as I was unsure what sanctions should follow worm eating. Would a trip to the office for First Aid be needed, or maybe even an emergency emetic?

"Good. It isn't very nice to eat worms, is it, Stephen?"

"No, Mrs Freeman," he answered. "That's why I was only sucking them."

The children Mrs Hall had taken to the local fire station had thoroughly enjoyed their field trip and the firefighters were enjoying answering the questions. "Could you please tell me," asked a six-year-old, "how you get back up the pole?"

A teacher was taking a group of pupils around Stonehenge when one of them said: "Miss, I was here three years ago and it hasn't changed much."

Jack Benny was very proud of the fact that a school in his home town of Waukegan, Illinois, was named after him, and used to return to speak to the children when in the neighbourhood. His speech concluded on one occasion, he

asked if there were any questions. "Mr Benny," one young pupil asked, "why did they name you after our school?"

The school team was about to be selected for the annual area swimming gala. All pupils in Years 3 to 6 were asked to stay behind after assembly for a meeting, when non-swimmers were then told they could go. Emma, a recent recruit to the school, burst into tears. After she had calmed down, she was asked the reason for the outburst: "I don't want to go. I really like this school." *(Steve Harrison)*

Q: What seven-letter word has three "u"s in it?
A: I really don't know, but it must be unusual. *(Henry O. Dormann)*

In 1983 on the tour of New Zealand and Australia, the Prince and Princess of Wales approached a group of young children in South Australia on one of their "walkabouts". The nearest child was patted on the head by Princess Diana. "Why aren't you at school today?" she enquired. "I've been sent home with head lice," replied the boy.

A small boy in a junior class was contentedly making a meal of some chewing-gum. Following an age-old school custom, his teacher commanded the offender to leave his seat and deposit the delicacy in the waste-paper basket. Peter emerged from his seat but on reaching the basket stood still and looked very much perturbed. Asked to explain, he answered pathetically: "I'll cop it, Miss, when I get home – my brother only lent me it for the afternoon."

Cheap. Electric guitar and powerful amplifier. Phone 536478. If boy answers please ring off and call later. *(Basingstoke)*

The teacher at a Durham school was becoming more and more irritated by Thomas who was continually sniffing. When she could stand it no longer she asked him: "Thomas, do you have a handkerchief?" Thomas replied: "Yes, Miss. Would you like to borrow it?"

Last night I was feeling very thirsty so I went downstairs for a drink of water. My mammy and daddy were lying on the carpet in front of the gas fire with nothing on – sunbathing. *(Little boy writing in his diary)*

The three-year-old told the childminder that her grandad had gone away in an aeroplane to Oil. It was only when her mother had come to collect her it was clarified that he had gone on his holidays to Greece.

Little girl: Mammy, how do the Spice Girls learn all the words to their songs?
Mother: Well, just like you learn all the words to your nursery rhymes.
Little girl: Oh, do they sit cross-legged on the carpet?

Q: What do you think is the best aspect of school meals?
A: Teachers have to suffer too.

Teacher: If all the good people in the world were red and all the bad people were green, what colour would you be?
Little girl: Miss, I think I'd be streaky.

When my son was eight years old he came home from school and announced he was in love, adding: "But I can't marry her. She's a Roman Catholic and I'm a prostitute." *(Letter in the Sunday Sun)*

A Fife teacher asked her class if any of them had been to Turkey. "Yes," one replied, "but we pronounce it 'Tor-kee'."

The school hall was full of children, staff, helpers and governors. The pantomime began. Soon the time came for Jack to go to market with the cow. He met "the baddie", who tricked him. If Jack could answer three questions, he would keep his mother's cow and get some money.

"What is your favourite colour?"

"Easy," said Jack. "Green."

"What is the capital of France?"

As quick as a flash, a voice piped up from among the six-year-old class at the back of the hall. "F – it's F," he shouted. "The capital of France is F. I know because I can spell it."

A class of six-year-olds had been learning about the "magic 'e'" ("win" becomes "wine", "tub" becomes "tube" . . .). The class had also had head lice. One of the pupils told his mother as she treated his hair not to worry as he could change his "nit" to "nite" with the magic "e".

Then there are those who are too clever by half . . .

Young scientist's rocket kit for sale, used once only. Also good home for only white mouse in neighbourhood which knows what it's like from 50ft up. *(San Francisco News)*

Little girl in her first year at secondary school to mother: Did you see my French teacher?
Mother: Miss Daneuve – yes, she was very nice.
Little girl: She's not a Miss, she's a Madam.

Prodigy – a child who plays the piano when he ought to be in bed.

And there are those who claim unhappy and poverty-stricken childhoods . . .

Eric: When I was eight I ran away with a circus.
Ernie: Really?
Eric: Yes. Then when I was nine, they made me bring it back again. *(Eric Morecambe and Ernie Wise)*

Ernie: I had a pretty tough childhood myself, you know. At the age of five I was left an orphan.
Eric: That's ridiculous! What could a five-year-old do with an orphan? *(Eric Morecambe and Ernie Wise)*

There are those who like to recall their impoverished background, remembering the days when they took their fish-paste sandwiches to school wrapped up in the waxed paper of Mother's Pride.

Heads will recollect at retirement celebrations such fictional observations about the retiree as . . .

He was so poor that one day his mam gave him a button and told him to nip next door to Mrs Bate's and ask her if she would put a shirt on it.

He was so poor he couldn't afford shoes – he set the boot studs into his feet.

One day he went to school with the sole of his boot hanging off. He met the head who took a bundle of notes secured with an elastic band from his pocket and gave him the elastic band to stop his sole flapping.

And what about Granny and Grandad . . .?

A grandmother is a lady who has no children of her own. She likes other people's little girls.

A grandfather is a man grandmother. He goes for walks with the boys and they talk about fishing, and tractors and things like that.

Grandmas don't have to do anything but be there.

They're old, so they shouldn't play or run. It is enough if they drive us to the market where the fairground is and have plenty of change in their pockets, or if they take us for walks, they should slow down past things like pretty leaves and caterpillars.

Usually they are fat but not too fat to tie our shoelaces.

Usually they wear glasses and funny underwear. They can take their teeth and gums out.

Everybody should try to have one, especially if they don't have a television, because grandmothers are the only grownups who have got the time.

5

Sport

We're going to have to use our heads a bit more when we bat. *(Nasser Hussain)*

Well Clive, it's all about the two M's. Movement and positioning. *(Ron Atkinson)*

If Glenn Hoddle said anything to his team at half time, it was concentration and focus. *(Ron Atkinson)*

Michael Owen – he's got the legs of a salmon. *(Craig Brown)*

I've seen some players with very big feet, and some with very small feet. *(David Pleat)*

Pires has got something about him: he can go both ways depending on who's facing him. *(David Pleat)*

Goalkeepers aren't born today until they're in their late twenties or thirties and sometimes not even then. *(Kevin Keegan)*

Chile have three options – they could win or they could lose. *(Kevin Keegan)*

I came to Nantes two years ago and it's much the same today, except that it's completely different. *(Kevin Keegan)*

Zidane is not very happy, because he's suffering from the wind. *(Kevin Keegan)*

Despite his white boots, he has pace and aggression. *(Kevin Keegan)*

In life he was a living legend; in death, nothing has changed. *(Barry Venison)*

When you're 4–0 up you should never lose 7–1. *(Lawrie McMenemy)*

Arnie Palmer, usually a great putter, seems to be having trouble with his long putts. However, he has no trouble dropping his shorts. *(US golf commentator)*

Billy Jean has always been conscious of wind on the centre court. *(Dan Maskell)*

Maradona gets tremendous elevation with his balls, no matter what position he's in. *(David Pleat)*

What I said to them at half time would be unprintable on the radio. *(Gerry Francis)*

Girls shouldn't play with men's balls – their hands are too small. *(Senator Wally Horn on basketball)*

The problem with intersexual swimming is that the boys often outstrip the girls.

Running is a unique experience, and I thank God for exposing me to the track team.

Gascoigne has pissed a fartness test. *(Bob Wilson)*

They're two points behind us so we're neck and neck. *(Bobby Robson)*

Apart from their goals, Norway haven't scored. *(Terry Venables)*

I think this could be our best victory over Germany since the war. *(John Motson)*

Bruce has got the taste of Wembley in his nostrils. *(John Motson)*

So different from the scenes in 1872, at the Cup Final none of us can remember. *(John Motson)*

Actually, none of the players are wearing earrings. Kjeldberg, with his contact lenses, is the closest we can get.' *(John Motson)*

As the four finalists hit the bend in the 1500 metres race, Thomson produced an electrifying bust which swept him past his opponents into the home straight to breast the tape. *(Camarthen Journal)*

Ampleforth elected to bath first on a pitch damp on top from the early rain. *(Wolverhampton Express and Star)*

I love sports. Whenever I can, I watch the Detroit Tigers on the radio. *(Gerald Ford)*

Sports Focus apologises for getting its wires crossed last week, and would like to make the following correction to the quote of the week: 'Saddam Hussain is not the England cricket captain – He is the leader of Iraq.' We meant to say 'Nasser Hussain'.

Front page sport

So who ever broke a leg at golf? ALAN SMITH EVERY SUNDAY *(The People)*

INJURY FORCES MISS TRUMAN TO SCRATCH *(Hartlepool Mail)*

MARY'S TWO BOOBS SINK BRITAIN *(The Sun)*

This does not detract from the achievements of the charging Eton bowler, whose balls came off the pitches so fast batsmen were hustled into errors. *(Marlborough Review)*

The most one-footed player since Long John Silver. *(Comment on Savo Milosevic in Birmingham Evening Mail)*

You are talking about a man who spelled his name wrong on his transfer request. *(West Brom manager Gary Megson on player Jason Roberts)*

As a small boy I was torn between two ambitions; to be a footballer or to run away and join a circus. At Partick Thistle I got to do both. *(Alan Hansen)*

Yurrrgggggh! *Der stod Ingelland!* Lord Nelson! Lord Beaverbrook! Winston Churchill! Henry Cooper! Clement Attlee! Anthony Eden! Lady Diana! *Der stod dem all! Der stod dem all!* Maggie Thatcher, can you hear me? Can you hear me, Maggie? Your boys took one hell of a beating tonight. *(Borg Lillelien, Norwegian commentator, Norway 2, England 1, 1981)*

ACLCOHOLISM V COMMUNISM *(Banner waved by Scotland fans versus the USSR, 1982)*

You could put his knowledge of the game on a postage stamp. He wanted us to sign Salford Van Hire because he thought he was a Dutch international. *(Fred Ayre on unnamed Wigan Athletic football director)*

Personally, I have always looked on cricket as organised loafing. *(Future Archbishop of Canterbury William Temple when he was Headmaster of Repton, c.1914)*

Cricket is the only game you can put on weight while playing. *(Tommy Docherty)*

It's a funny kind of month, October. For the keen cricket fan it's when you realise your wife left you in May. *(Denis Norden)*

Grandmother or tails, sir? *(Anonymous rugby referee to Princess Anne's son Peter Phillips, Gordonstoun School's rugby captain, at pre-match coin toss)*

Chairman of the Bored *(Comment by The Herald Sun, Sydney, on Clive Woodward)*

James Dudgeon of Lincoln City was sent off for a booable offence. *(Grimsby Sports Telegraph)*

I would like to thank the press from the heart of my bottom. *(Nick Faldo after winning the Open in 1992)*

Ernie: You know what your main trouble is?
Eric: What?
Ernie: You stand too close to the ball after you've hit it.

Tiger Woods won his first international tournament at the age of eight. This was not his first tournament victory, however. That came in a ten-and-under tournament – when Tiger was two years old.

And now over to ringside, where Harry Commentator is your carpenter. *(Unknown BBC link-up man)*

Sure there have been injuries and deaths in boxing, but none of them serious. *(Alan Minter)*

Tommy Cooper: I was in the ring once with Cassius Clay, and I got him worried.
Henry Cooper: Oh, really?
Tommy Cooper: He thought he'd killed me.

If you want to see what you'll look like in another ten years, look in the mirror after you've run a marathon. *(Jeff Scaff)*

And the line-up for the final of the women's 400 metres hurdles includes three Russians, two East Germans, a Pole, a Swede and a Frenchman. *(David Coleman)*

Zola Budd: so small, so waif-like, you literally can't see her. But there she is. *(Alan Parry)*

I was watching Sumo wrestling on the television for two hours before I realised it was darts. *(Hattie Hayridge, comedienne)*

This is really a lovely horse. I once rode her mother. *(Ted Walsh, commentator)*

My word, look at that magnificent erection! *(Brough Scott on the new stand at the Doncaster course)*

Willie Carson, riding his 180th winner of the season, spent the last two furlongs looking over one shoulder then another, even between his legs, but there was nothing there to worry him. *(Sporting Life)*

I backed a horse today at five to one – it came in at ten past four. *(Tommy Cooper)*

And the victorious crew celebrate in the traditional manner – dipping their cox into the Thames. *(The Guardian)*

I am getting to the age when I can only enjoy the last sport left. It is called 'hunting for your spectacles'. *(Sir Edward Grey)*

And finally . . .

A local junior football coach in the northeast of England used the same opening speech every year: 'We have to act as sportsmen at all times. There will be no yelling at the referees or other players and no being poor losers. Is that understood?' At that point the kids would nod, then the coach would add, 'Good. Now, please go home and explain all that to your parents.'

6

Job Opportunities

WANTED – Some additional female technicians at the fast-expanding Charles River Breeding Laboratory. No previous experience necessary. (*Advert in Massachusetts paper*)

Glamour photographer with own equipment and good contacts seeks sleeping or active partner. (*Advert in The Stage*)

WANTED – Solicitor, experienced in laundry or dye works, to drive wagon. (*Vancouver World*)

Donald's father told the court that his son's personality had completely changed since the accident. His career in the catering industry was finished because of it and he carried a chip on his shoulder.

Job Opportunities for Those with Earning Disabilities. (*South Manchester Reporter*)

COOK WANTED – March 1st. Comfortable room with radio; two in family; only one who can be well recommended. (*Advert in Hereford Paper*)

Lady with one child, two-and-a-half years old, seeks situation as housekeeper. oGod cook. *(Advert in S. African Paper)*

A brown snake bit reptile-collector Neville Burns, 19, in Sydney yesterday – and dropped dead. *(The People)*

WANTED URGENTLY – Male or Female serving person for top London nightclub. Must fit uniform 40" bust. *(New Evening Standard)*

Nursing sister Patricia Gregan had six double Scotches at a hotel and missed her train home. So she went by goods train – riding thirty miles astride the couplings between two trucks. Part of the ride was through a mile and a half long tunnel. Today in a Sydney court 54-year-old Mrs Gregan was charged with travelling on a portion of a goods train not intended for passengers and with being on railway property while intoxicated. She admitted both offences and was fined £200. Mrs Gregan said: 'It was a terrifying experience.' She promised she would not do it again. *(Daily Mail)*

Miss Georgina P. Mason, psychologist, quoted the case of a nine-year-old boy who ran amok with a hatchet in the large family of which he was a member, saying, 'There are far too many bairns here.' She showed how by psychological treatment he became completely adjusted and several years later was working a guillotine in a printer's establishment. *(Ross-shire Journal)*

Friends' Academy, Locust Valley, Long Island, Co-educational, with special opportunities for boys. *(Friend's Intelligencer)*

Girl wanted for petrol pump attendant. *(Advert in Oxford Mail)*

A circus man in Bor, Yugoslavia, who has already eaten more than 22,500 razor blades, a ton of brassware, cutlery, nuts, bolts and assorted ironware, has now bought himself a bus – which he intends to eat within the next two years. *(Sunday Mirror)*

Youth wanted – To train as Petrol Pump Attendant. 5-day week, Mon. to Sat., 9–6 p.m. Elderly man would suit. *(Bantry)*

RECREATION DEPARTMENT: Borough of Richmond Requires An Assistant Cemeteries Superintendent.

LAKER AIRWAYS – CABIN STAFF. Staff required for Gatwick Base. All applicants must be between 20 and 33 years of age. Height 5'4" to 5'10". Education GCSE standard. Must be able to swim. *(Luton Gazette)*

A new £2,500,000 sewage treatment works for Chipping Norton got under way on Monday when County Councillor Oliver Colston performed a brief inaugural ceremony.
(Oxford Journal)

Part-time Job – An unexpected vacancy for a KNIFE THROWER'S ASSISTANT *(Milton Keynes Gazette)*

Some people are being overcharged on funeral costs, the Lord Mayor of Norwich, Mr Ralph Roe, told the city's Health Committee yesterday. 'Some people are being taken for a ride,' Mr Roe commented. *(Eastern Daily Press)*

Brief details regarding conditions of service are set out in the attached copy letter headed 'Walk Tall with the City of London Special Constabulary'. Members of staff who are interested should either call, write or telephone giving details of age, height and occupation to: Mr. K. Short, City of London Special Constabulary.

'I soon hope to offer body piercing and chiropody but I'm just trying to find my feet at the moment . . .' *(Dewsbury Reporter)*

It was thought that he might follow in his father's footsteps and become a butcher and slaughterer but he soon left and joined the 1st Battalion of the Middlesex Regiment. *(Wembley News)*

SERVANT GIRL WANTED for country surgeon's home. £130 per week and the use of Harmonium on Sundays. Plymouth sister preferred. *(Pulse)*

YOUNG POULTRY MAN – A young poultry man, who is keen to climb the tree and already knows his work, is required immediately in Southern Africa. A good salary is offered with free passage and housing, and, for a bachelor, a servant to boot. *(Poultry World)*

FALKLAND ISLANDS – There are vacancies for TWO CAMP TEACHERS in the Falkland Islands Education Department. Candidates must be unmarried men. *(Observer)*

H.M. PRISON WAKEFIELD require a SEMI-SKILLED LABOURER. An ability to erect small scaffolds will be an advantage. *(Pontefract & Castleford Express)*

Why is it, I wonder, that butchers always seem cheerful? It is not that their job is a particularly enviable one, for in cold weather meat must be very cold to handle. Maybe they get rid of any bad temper by bashing away with their choppers. *(Woman's Own)*

Wanted – Chambermaid in rectory. Love in, 200 dollars a month. *(US paper)*

Wanted: First class male waitress. Only qualified persons considered.

Wanted – Unmarried girls to pick fresh fruit and produce at night.

A young woman wants washing and cleaning daily. *(Toronto Times)*

Wanted – Men to take care of cows that do not smoke or drink.

Wanted – Mother's help. Peasant working conditions.

Wanted – Widower with school age children requires person to assume general housekeeping duties. Must be capable of contributing to the growth of the family.

Wanted – Preparer of food. Must be dependable, like the food business and be willing to get his hands dirty. *(Baltimore Sun)*

When I was a child, what I wanted to be when I was grown up was an invalid. *(Quentin Crisp)*

He's been on the dole so long he goes to the staff dances. *(Bobby Thompson)*

He had ambitions, at one time, to become a sex maniac, but he failed his practical. *(Les Dawson)*

A good farmer is nothing more nor less than a handy man with a sense of humus. *(E.B. White)*

My friend, the undertaker, the last person on earth to let me down.

A married man must love his wife but a navvy can have his pick. *(Max Miller)*

Have you ever fallen out of a patient? *(Groucho Marx to a tree surgeon)*

The reason why we can sell our antiques for less is because we buy them direct from the manufacturer. *(Antique dealer advertising in the Washington Times)*

Work Place Graffiti

Yesterday I couldn't spell engineer.
Now I are one

You Can Tell A British Workman By His Hands . . .
- They are always in his pockets

7

Medicine

Mountains of beef and butter are hard to swallow.

Disadvantages of sexual reproduction: The majority of humans tend to mate with species of their own sort.

These colours are detected by colons in the eyes.

Each woman ought to examine her breast or any other abominations.

In arthritis joints may cease up.

The symptoms of influenza are similar to those of flu.

The immune system is easily weekend.

People with diabetes must take insulin everyday with a needle. Some people need multiple erections everyday for diabetes. Most people with diabetes learn to give themselves erections.

Signs and symptoms of arthritis: joints all rusty.

The parents can decide on whether to have children or not.

While in Accident and Emergency, she was examined, x-rated and then sent home.

The skin was moist and dry.

The patient was alert and unresponsive.

Rectal examination revealed an active thyroid.

She stated that she had been constipated most of her life until she got a divorce.

Madame Curie invented the radiator.

I saw your patient today and she is staying under the car of the consultant for physical therapy.

Examination of genitalia revealed he is circus sized.

The patient refused an autopsy.

The patient has no previous history of suicide.

She has no rigors or shaking but her husband says that she was very hot in bed last night.

On the second day the knee felt better and on the third it disappeared completely.

She is numb from her toes down.

To be a good nurse you must be completely sterile.

It is a misconception for pregnant women to believe that alcohol has no effect on the unborn foetus.

The leopard has black spots on its body which look like sores – those who catch sores get leprosy.

Human beings share a need of food, shelter and sex with lower animals.

Medicine plus

Specialist in women and other diseases. *(Doctor's clinic in Rome)*

Do not drive car or operate machinery *(On Boot's children's cough medicine)*

Widow In Bed With A Case Of Salmon *(Liverpool Echo)*

So I went to the doctor's and he said, 'You've got hypochondria.' I said, 'Not that as well.' *(Tim Vine)*

'Bodies in the garden are a plant,' says wife. *(Hong Kong Standard)*

IF YOU HAVE NOT HAD YOUR FLU SHOT THIS YEAR, ASK YOUR DOCTOR OR NURSE TO GET ONE. *(Notice in a hospital)*

TB or not TB, that is the congestion. *(Woody Allen)*

Transplant Man Dies – Dusan Vlaco, from Yugoslavia, the second-longest surviving heart transplant patient, has died in Los Angeles. He received the transplant on September 18th, 1698. *(Belfast Telegraph)*

To prevent contraception: wear a condominium.

Rib ticklers

I met a guy this morning who had a glass eye – he didn't tell me, it just came out in the conversation. *(Jerry Dennis)*

Doctor: I don't like the look of your husband.
Wife: I don't either, but he's good to the children.

I went to the doctor and I said, 'It hurts me when I do that.' He said, 'Well, don't do it.' *(Tommy Cooper)*

Doctor: You're going to live until you are eighty.
Patient: I am eighty.
Doctor: What did I tell you?

First you forget names, then you forget faces, then you forget to pull your zipper up, then you forget to pull your zipper down. *(Leo Rosenberg)*

She got her looks from her father – he's a plastic surgeon. *(Groucho Marx)*

The doctor called the plumber out late on Saturday night because his lavatory cistern was not flushing. The plumber took two aspirins out of his pocket and put them down the toilet. When the doctor protested, the plumber said, 'You know the routine – if it's no better in the morning, give me a call.'

I got the bill for my surgery. Now I know why those doctors were wearing masks. *(J. Boren)*

Doctor: I'm afraid you're dying.
Patient: How long have I got?
Doctor: Ten . . .

Patient: Ten what? Ten weeks, ten days?
Doctor: Ten, nine, eight, seven . . .

A man went to the doctor's with a cucumber in his left ear, a carrot in his right ear and a banana up his nose. 'What's wrong with me?' he asked. 'Simple,' said the doctor, 'You're not eating properly.'

A woman went to the doctor's clutching the side of her face. 'What seems to be the problem?' asked the doctor. 'Well,' said the woman, removing her hand, 'it's this pimple on my cheek. There's a small tree growing from it, and a table and chairs, and a picnic basket. What on earth can it be?' 'It's nothing to worry about,' said the doctor. 'It's only a beauty spot.'

Medical Officer: How are your bowels working?
Recruit: Haven't been issued with any sir.
M.O.: I mean are you constipated?
Recruit: No, sir, I volunteered.
M.O.: For goodness sake man, don't you know the King's English.
Recruit: No, sir, is he?

Medical graffiti

DOCTORS' LOUNGE
– and they get paid for it
(St Thomas's hospital, London)

Is a Buddhist Monk refusing an injection at the dentist's trying to transcend dental medication?

AMNESIA RULES, O . . .

Give blood – play hockey

MEDICAL TERMINOLOGY – CHILDREN'S STYLE

Barium – What doctors do when their patients pass away

Bowel – A letter like A I O U

Caesarean Section – A neighbourhood in Rome

Coma – Punctuation mark

Dilate – Live longer

Fibula – A small lie

Genital – Not a Jew

Impotent – Distinguished, well-known

Morbid – A higher offer

Rectum – Dang nearly killed 'em

Varicose – Nearby

Vein – conceited

8

Things They Thought They Heard

Thanks to a number of factors – the limited vocabulary of small youngsters, indistinct and poorly articulated speech and the mixture of music with lyrics amongst them – children can easily put their own interpretations on the spoken word, as these examples show . . .

There is a phrase in the Beatles' song "Lucy In The Sky With Diamonds" which goes ". . . the girl with kaleidoscope eyes". A young pupil was convinced it went ". . . the girl with colitis goes by".

A young boy called his teddy bear "Gladly" because of the line from the hymn which sounds like: "Gladly, my cross-eyed bear . . ." (Gladly, my cross I bear . . .)

Our Father, chart in heaven, hullo how be you then?

Our Father, who aren't in heaven, hello, what's your name?

Our Father, who art in heaven, Harold be thy name.

Our Father, who art in heaven, how d'you know my name?

. . . and lead us not into Penn Station.

A little girl returned home to tell her mam that her elder sister would be late. She had been selected as a prostitute for the netball team.

All things bright and beautiful, All teachers great and small.

Surely good Mrs Murphy shall follow me all the days of my life. (Surely goodness and mercy shall follow me . . .)

Blessed art thou a monk's women. (Blessed art thou amongst women.)

A whale in a manger.

The Russians revolted and overthrew Nicholas II who was bizarre. (. . . who was the Tsar.)

Mrs Gulliver, from Barnard Castle, County Durham, recalls a story told to her by an elderly friend. When, as a schoolgirl, her friend, fellow classmates and teacher had to sing the National Anthem, she was always puzzled by the phrase "send him victorious". She asked her teacher whether the King really liked plums because she had only greengages in her garden and could she send them some of them rather than Victorias.

It ordipends on what you think.

I have unopened mind about that.

Every sentence and the name of God must begin with a caterpillar.

While shepherds washed their socks by night . . .

Jesus said to His disciples: "Follow Me and I will make you vicious old men."

I know that my reindeer liveth. (. . . Redeemer liveth.)

Hail! Thou that art highly-flavoured. (. . . highly favoured.)

Rachel will have to work hard next term if she is to be sure of a GCSE in June. A lot of his mistakes are due to carelessness.

A Hampshire reader insists that under "Headmaster's Comments" in her nine-year-old son's report are the words: "Unimaginative but reliable. Would make a good parent."

This boy listens in school with the flawless dignity of the dead.

Not a very good set of reports, but don't take too much notice of them – two of them, I know, were written by tired men.

COMMENT: (DO TAKE THIS OPPORTUNITY FOR EXPRESSING ANY CONCERNS YOU MAY HAVE . . .) I think I can do better if he tries.

To be charitable, let us say it was a Freudian slip when a Sussex teacher wrote on a pupil's report that his "excuses are always interesting and varied. I am, however, running out of patients."

Alan is producing his best work . . . alas.

George has told me he wants to pass his exams badly – I can assure you he is going the right way about it.

Thomas's handwriting is so bad we cannot tell if he can spell or not.

William is very intelligent but his handwriting is atrocious. Would make a good doctor.

Bernard's idea of hard work is sharpening his pencil and putting his books away.

I can only hope that should Charles ever have children, they give him the same experience that as a child he has given me!

Regan writes well, spells well and has a fertile imagination which, unfortunately, is sometimes matched by an overuse of earthy language.

Jenny is a clever girl and wants to go into bonking.

His work is as sloppy as a soup sandwich.

I received David's report and agree with you that he is bone idle. I don't know why it is – I think he takes after his mother whose father used to say as a child she had swallowed a teaspoon and hasn't stirred since.

9

School Matters

Headteacher bloopers

Don't let worry kill you – let the school help.

Because of the large number of examinations in the hall today, children will be examined at both ends.

Remember to offer your prayers for the many who are sick of our school community.

After assembly on Thursday afternoon there will be a Year 6 ice-cream party. Would Miss Thomas, Mrs Franklin and Mrs George, who are providing the milk, please meet at lunch time.

Because Sunday is Easter Day, Sophie Briggs from Form 8D will come onto the stage and lay an egg on the table.

A 'Beans and Sausage' supper will take place in the hall on Thursday and this will be followed by music.

Mr Evans, the head teacher, spoke briefly, much to the delight of his audience.

Years 9,10 and 11 will be presenting 'Hamlet' next Friday in the school hall and all pupils are encouraged to buy tickets at the office for this tragedy.

In a word – I don't think so.

I would like to thank all of you children for your prayers for the recovery of our deputy head Mrs Hall – God is good, Mrs Hall is better.

The head of the PTA gave the school secretary the list of prizes for the raffle to be typed and amongst the list was the item 'large cans of lager'. The secretary gave the list to the head teacher who asked, 'What happened to the large candelabra?'

If you can't imitate him, then don't copy him.

For your information, just answer me one question.

I'm willing to admit that I may not always be right, but I'm never wrong.

Secretary: Should I destroy these ten-year-old records?
Head teacher: Yes, but make copies.

True, I have taken a long time to give you a 'yes' or 'no' – but now I'm giving you a definite maybe.

Never make forecasts about the future.

Put it out of your mind – soon it will be a forgotten memory.

Who is sitting in the empty chair?

We note with regret that Mrs Calhoun is recuperating from an automobile accident.

In the Sixth Form we've been trying to get uniform done away with. I think we'll soon be down to the boys just wearing a tie and the girls a grey skirt.

Ladies who have kindly undertaken to act as school crossing wardens are reminded again that if they attempt to carry out their duties without their clothing on motorists are unlikely to take any notice of them. *(Circular to school parents)*

Mr. E.G. Winterton, head teacher, would not comment on the threat. However, he did say, 'Some children have been behaving very childishly.' *(Doncaster Post)*

Today was the first day for nine days that some pupils have been able to use their toilets. We must do something to relieve this situation. *(From the head teacher's report to governors)*

Teachers who wish to have typing done should take advantage of the female staff in the main office.

I would like to remind staff that I shall take as long as is required to make a snap decision.

The after-lunch talk was given by Mr Derek Wigram – school head teacher, retired, but now serving the Lord in an advisory capacity. *(Crusade)*

Winners in the Parents' Association home-made wine competition were Mrs Davis (fruity, well-rounded), Mrs

Raynor (fine colour and full-bodied), and Miss Ogle- Smith (slightly acid, but should improve if laid down). *(Head teacher's circular)*

The head teacher of King James' School will preach at the Parish Church on Sunday, May 13th, and another of the staff on May 6th. On both these Sundays I hope to be away on holiday. *(Vicar's announcement in St Mary the Virgin's parish newsletter)*

Will those teachers wishing for leave of absence to attend the funeral of a grandmother or other close relative please inform the Head before 12 noon on the day of the match.

The head teacher said that they still had piles to deal with. *(Staff circular re: exam papers)*

I know you believe you understand what you think I said, but I am not sure you realise that what you heard is not what I meant. *(Head teacher at staff meeting)*

Will the individual who borrowed a ladder from the care-taker last month kindly return same immediately, other-wise further steps will be taken. *(Head teacher's request to staff in Derbyshire)*

Comments from references from head teachers:

Mr Bingham has worked for me for fifteen years and when he left I was perfectly satisfied.

If you can get Mr George to work for you, you will indeed be fortunate.

And observations from CVs received by head teachers:

My intensity and focus are at inordinately high levels, and my ability to complete projects on time is unspeakable.

Education: Curses in liberal arts, curses in computer science, curses in accounting.

Personal: Married, 1992 Chevrolet.

I have an excellent track record, although I am not a horse.

I am a rabid typist.

Proven ability to track down and correct erors.

Personal interests: Donating blood. 15 gallons so far.

References: None, I've left a path of destruction behind me.

Strengths: Ability to meet deadlines while maintaining composer.

Don't take the comments of my former employer too seriously, they were unappreciative beggars and slave drivers.

Extensive background in accounting. I can also stand on my head!

And from the covering letter . . .

Thank you for your consideration. Hope to hear from you shorty.

And if you make it as far as the interview . . .

The young teacher was asked at his interview what particular role he had played as 'Local co-ordinator of regional media distribution', a post he had included in his CV. 'To be perfectly honest,' he replied, 'for a couple of years I was Head Paper Boy.'

In the interview they put me up against a woman and it was a case of touch and go.

Staff graffiti

Our Headteacher has shoes so shiny I can see my face in them

The wages of sin is death but the wages here are a lot worse

SCHOOL MATTERS IN PRINT

MEDINA TO HAVE PARENT TEACHER ASSASSINA-TION *(Headline in Medina Sentinel)*

Councillor Mrs Hallinan said the education authority had set up various nits in different parts of Cardiff. *(South Wales Echo)*

John Fisher, the student star of St George's College Christmas concert, was in a car accident last week. However, we are happy to state that he will still be able to appear this evening in four pieces. *(Durham Advertiser)*

Formerly a don at Oxford, he developed later an interest in education, and migrated to Ontario. *(Canadian Review)*

The winner of St Patrick's competition to guess the number of sweets in the jar was Mrs Linden, who will therefore travel to Majorca by air, spend five days in a luxury hotel (all inclusive) and fly home via Paris, without any need to spend a penny. *(Announcement in a Westmoreland church magazine)*

Nineteen-year-old Texan student Roger Martinez set a world record by swallowing 225 live goldfish in 42 minutes in a San Antonio contest. His prize: a free fish dinner. *(Sun)*

The nearest school is over five miles away in one direction and practically twelve miles in the opposite direction. *(Ulster Magazine and Eire Review)*

Apart from an isolated incident of violence in 1470 when the dean of the faculty of arts was shot at with bows and arrows, and if one glosses over the Jacobite demonstrations of 1715, the university has been singularly free of student unrest. *(From prospectus of St Andrew's University)*

The first hearing was adjourned to enable the students to be regally represented. *(Surrey Advertiser)*

Martin C—, aged 63, a retired teacher, was said by a police officer at Clerkenwell, last week, to have walked along Randolph Road, Camden Town, 'absolutely nude' on Sunday afternoon, shouting: 'How about this, then?' *(North London Press)*

These are some of the pictures on show at the Young Artists' Exhibition in Moscow's Central Exhibition Hall, one of the USSR's 50th Anniversary events. The 1,500 exhibits, displayed to the best advantage over nearly two acres, are the pick of 20,000 submitted by young painters, graphic artists and sculptors in every Soviet Republic. Nearly all were executed over the past two years. *(Soviet Weekly)*

Mr Wedgwood Benn said: '. . . there is a great revolution under way in education. My education policy is to raise the school leaving age to 65.' *(Evening Post)*

Letters from The Times:

Sir,

I possess an unused pre-stamped postcard that was issued to me when I first went to camp as a member of the Boys' Brigade in 1943. Headed 'CAMP (labour saving) POST CARD' it incorporates a 'tick or delete' list which included:

Dear Mum/Dad/Uncle/Aunt/Old Thing;

I am . . . In the pink/In clink/Having a gorgeous time/Starving/Home sick.

The weather is . . . Fine/Wet/Below zero/Tropical.

My money is . . . Spent/Given to charity/In the canteen/Have plenty.

Please send me . . . A clean shirt/Nourishing food/A return ticket/Your love.

Camp is . . . Wonderful/Horrible/Going too quickly/Not 'arf alright.

Your loving . . . Son/Nephew/Pal.

Sir,

To get your offspring to communicate when they are away, write to them, ending the letter: 'I hope the enclosed cheque is of some use', but without enclosing anything.

You will get a phone call the next day.

Sir,

Our understanding daughter had a rubber stamp made for her younger brother when he was at university. It read: 'Date as postmark. Dear Mum and Dad. Still alive. All is well. Love George.'

School graffiti

WET PAINT
This is <u>not</u> an instruction!

The Graffiti in this school is terrible - and so are the dinners

Examinations - Natures Laxative
(London Poly.)

Education kills by degrees
(Newcastle University)

Don't let them cut hire education
(Camberwell School)

Road safety notice outside of Junior School:
Drive carefully. Don't kill a child.
Wait for a teacher

10

Facts of Life

Bigamy is having one husband too many. Monogamy is the same.

You've got to be married, haven't you? You can't go through life being happy. *(Colin Crompton)*

The only reason I would take up jogging is so that I could hear heavy breathing again. *(Erma Bombeck)*

Contraceptives should be used on every conceivable occasion. *(Spike Milligan)*

When Lady Astor was canvassing for her first parliamentary seat in Plymouth, a senior naval officer was appointed to accompany her as she went around town knocking on doors. One door was opened by a small girl. 'Is your mother at home?' Lady Astor inquired. 'No,' the child replied, 'but she said if a lady comes with a sailor, they're to use the upstairs room and leave ten bob.'

Facts of life from the press

It is strictly forbidden on our Black Forest camping site that people of different sex, for instance men and women, live together in one tent unless they are married with each other for that purpose. The meaning of this regulation is that otherwise the purpose of the furlough, namely, recreation, could not be guaranteed. *(Caravan Club Magazine)*

Mordell Lecture. Professor J. Tits, of the College de France, will deliver the Mordell Lecture at 5 p.m. on Monday, 24 April in the Babbage Lecture Theatre, New Museums Site. The title of the lecture will be 'Rigidity'. *(Cambridge University)*

BRONTE COTTAGE – 17th Century luxury cottage. Ideal honeymoon. Sleeps 2/5. *(The Times)*

Mr E. Brien – In a report last week of a court case involving Mr Edward Brien of Scottes Lane, Dagenham, we wrongly stated that Mr Brien had previously been found guilty of buggery. The charge referred to was, in fact, one of burglary. *(Dagenham Post)*

According to the complaint, Mrs O'Donnell told the court her husband started amusing her three days before the marriage. *(Texas Clarion)*

Sheer stockings, designed for fancy dress, but so serviceable that lots of women wear nothing else. *(Advert)*

Girls for Boys' School – A school for boys, Sexey's School, Lusty Hill, Bruton, Somerset, is to take 22 girl pupils in September. *(The Times)*

She was married in Evansville, Indiana, to Walter Jackson, and to this onion was born three children. *(Ohio Paper)*

Student Derek Sydney Szuilmowski, aged 20, was wearing a skirt, cardigan, underslip, two pairs of tights, panties, and a bra when he sped through Camp Street shortly after midnight, it was stated at Salford. *(Manchester Evening News)*

The new chairman of the South East London Family Planning Association is Mrs Mary Walker, who is expecting a baby in a month's time. *(Croyden Advertiser)*

'Honeymoon? If we can fit it in,' say couple. *(Northern Echo)*

Mounting problems for young couples. *(Western Gazette)*

A study of 13,000 college students found that those given free condoms in giveaway programmes did not engage in more sex than others, and that the notion was unfounded. But they did douse more people with water balloons from their upper-floor dormitory windows. *(From the American Journal of Public Health)*

Miss Giavollela had pleaded guilty to stealing goods worth £25.10 from Tesco Supermarket; to assaulting a police-woman; and to dishonestly handling a garden gnome. *(Oxford Mail)*

Drive carefully in the New Year. Remember nine out of ten people are caused by accidents. *(Falkirk Herald)*

The judge said that when the school organist started to spend a lot of time at the rectory, Mr James warned his wife 'not to get into a position from which it might be difficult to withdraw'. *(Evening Standard)*

Retired teacher Aubrey Westlake is fed up with people asking if his caravan site and holiday centre is a nudist colony; 79-year-old Dr Westlake and his 72-year-old wife, Marjorie, cannot understand what makes people think their 'Sandy Balls Holiday Centre' is for nudists. *(The Sun)*

On Wednesday the 23rd (No Communion Service), the Vicar is conducting a Quiet Day for 40 pupils (recently confirmed) from Brentwood School. The Mothers' Union are catering for their physical needs, which are great. *(Roydon Parish Magazine)*

Your own LOG SAUNA for as little as £650 (plus erection). *(local paper)*

7.25 THE SAINT
Girls! Have you ever wondered what Roger Moore's legs look like? Now is your chance, for in this episode he wears the kilt! And that is not the only thing to watch for. *(TV Times)*

26th October – R.D. Smith has one sewing machine for sale. Phone 46379 after 7 p.m. and ask for Mrs Kelly who lives with him – cheap.

27th October – R.D. Smith informs us he has received several annoying telephone calls because of an incorrect ad in yesterday's paper. It should have read: R.D. Smith has one sewing machine for sale. Cheap. Phone 46379 after 7 p.m. and ask for Mrs Kelly who loves him.

28th October – R.D. Smith. We regret an error in R.D. Smith's classified advertisement yesterday. It should have read: R.D. Smith has one sewing machine for sale. Cheap. Phone 46379 and ask for Mrs Kelly who lives with him after 7 p.m. *(Tanganika Standard)*

Mr Charles Narrow, 23, yesterday obtained a divorce from his wife, Sissy, a 16-year-old Sixth Former, on the grounds of extreme cruelty, barely six months after their controversial wedding at a Florida nudist camp. He said she was cold and indifferent after the first three weeks of marriage. The daughter of a nudist camp proprietor, Sissy wore only a veil and a necklace at her wedding. *(News of the World)*

The judge said: 'There was a succession of boyfriends. Each time she would trundle her bed into the kitchen, shut the door and remain there for a substantial time. Then the man would leave and she would trundle the bed back into the bedroom and go to sleep. This must have been extremely embarrassing for her husband. It is possible she just wanted to sit and chat to the boyfriends and took the bed in because of the lack of furniture,' said the judge. *(The Sun)*

No Thanks
So – an American doctor thinks that men of sixty years of age should have two wives, does he? Well, I for one wouldn't want a dirty old man of sixty to share with some other woman - thank you very much!
Mrs N.G. Ewell, Surrey. *(The Sunday Mirror)*

SECRETARY WANTED – Spiritual Healer requires secretary to help cope with large male. Must be good at composing letters. Top salary to right person. *(Psychic News)*

CHEERFUL Lady Companion required in Bath. *(Bath & Wilts. Evening Chronicle)*

Sir,
A few weeks ago, my husband and I went to a party in Neasden, being given by my husband's boss, an insurance broker. The door was opened by the boss's wife, who, much

to my husband's astonishment and my shock, wasn't wearing a stitch of clothing. I was embarrassed, distressed and angry, but what can you do when your husband's boss and his wife are involved? I pretended not to notice a thing. *(Men Only)*

Sir,
I am not a Welsh teacher, but I love my country and my language very dearly. Learning Welsh at school did me no harm, as I received equal marks in both languages (full marks). I think that Welsh is far more pleasant and useful than sex, of which many people seem to get so much nowadays. *(Liverpool Daily Post)*

A young Russian man who dressed in women's clothes to sit an exam for his sister was caught by guards suspicious of his 'unusually prominent' bust and heavy make-up, Yasen Zasursky, dean of Moscow State University's journalism faculty, told Interfax news agency. *(Reuters)*

Facts of life – graffiti

(On back of unwashed white van)
Make Love - Not War
See driver for details!

My husband's a
marvellous lover
- He knows all my
erroneous zones.

Women like the simpler things in life - like men

My sister uses massacre on her eyes

THE ARMY BUILDS MEN
- PLEASE COULD THEY BUILD ME ONE, VERONICA?

8 out of every 10 men
write with a ball-point pen
- what do the other 2 do with it?

(Notice in Gents' toilet, Old Trafford)
Please adjust dress before leaving -
I don't wear a dress

Do you have a drink problem? – Yes,
I can't afford it.

Make Love not war - I'm married – I do both

Sex Is Bad For One - **but it's very good for two**

(Road sign)
SOFT SHOULDERS -
but warm thighs

Free Women - **where?**

Support wild life – **vote for an orgy** *(Oxford)*

Sex Appeal - please give generously

**Grow your own dope – plant a man
(On rear window of woman's car)**

11

Letters

The majority of letters arriving in schools from parents are usually excuses or explanations for a situation which has happened, or is going to happen . . .

Dear Sir/Miss . . .

Please excuse John from school today as his father's ill and the pig has to be fed.

I have some good and bad news for you. First of all, the good news – I will be taking my son away on Friday. Now the bad news – he will return in time for school on Monday.

Maryann was absent December 11-16, because she had a fever, sore throat, headache and upset stomach. Her sister was also sick, fever and sore throat, her brother had a low grade fever and ached all over. I wasn't the best either, sore throat and fever. There must be something going around, her father even got hot last night.

Sorry Kevin was late but me and my husband rather overdone it this morning.

John will be off until Friday. He has a cole slaw on his top lip.

You remember all the nose bleeds George has been having and made him stay off school? Well, the doctor is having him taken into hospital to have his nose circumcised. So that should be the end of his problem.

Sorry Mary wasn't at school yesterday but she had dire rear.

My son is under a doctor's care and should not take P.E. today. Please execute him.

Fiona will not be in school tomorrow. In the morning she is having a bath, then we are going to the hairdresser's and then to a dinner-dance at the club until 11.30 pm. I hope this is all right.

Sorry Anne was absent from school but she had an ulster in her throat.

Even though Jane left early for the bus, she had to come back with her stomach.

Elizabeth has been absent because her mother has had twins. I can assure you it will not happen again.

I am sorry that my son is late in handing in his homework. Yesterday morning when he had to hand it in, he had to go to hospital with his foot. He has brought it with him this morning.

I am asking you not to use corporal punishment on George. We never do except in self-defence.

John was off with information of the lungs.

I have kept Kevin off school because the doctor says he has slipped his dick.

Jennifer will not attend school for the next few weeks as we are going on holiday. I hope this does not interfere with your plans for industrial action or anything.

Dear School: Please excuse John being absent on Jan. 28, 29, 30, 31, 32, and also 33.

Joanne won't be in school for a few days because she's got trouble with her eye. The doctor thinks it's a misplaced rectum.

I'm sorry Ernie has not been to school all week, but we had a week last week I can tell you. On Monday, our Ernie broke his collar-bone and ended up in hospital; on Tuesday, Auntie Florrie collapsed and died at the club; and on Friday, I won £10 on the bingo. Isn't it funny how things always seem to happen in threes?

Brian was absent from school because he went to his grandmother's funeral. He stayed the night at his cousin's and he didn't come home on Tuesday because he had a hangover from drinking too much at the party afterwards.

Sorry Victor could not attend school yesterday as we had no sugar for his breakfast cup of tea.

Emily was not in school yesterday because my brain was disengaged. I thought it was half term.

Please excuse Jimmy for being. It was his father's fault.

Some parents seem to believe anything . . .

Angela did not come home till gone 11.30 last night, and I can't think where she'd got to but when she came in she was covered from head to foot with straw.

Guy couldn't come back to school yesterday as his mother was ill. There is no way he went to see *Grease*.

It was true what Harry told you. He was in the fish and chip shop when some of your pupils came in and battered him. I was amazed that Kirk obtained an 'A' for his Home

Economics – even the dog would not eat the scones he brought home.

Billy wasn't in school this morning because he looked after me when I went to get my eternity allowance.

Please send me a form for free dinners for children at reduced prices.

My daughter was absent yesterday because she was tired. She spent a weekend with the Marines.

My husband will not be able to come to the parents' meeting this afternoon because as you know he is in prison. He is not very happy with Richard's report and wants him to be disciplined.

Thank you for your letter on the arrangements for Entrance Appeals. We shall waste no time in reading it.

I'm pleased you are keeping Moira in detention. I think it will have a sanitary effect on her.

Very sorry Sharon has been absent again but she is very poorly with flu – could you please see that she is raped up warm at breaktime.

I kept Michael off school for his breathing again as he never gets any sleep with it when it comes on.

Ernest has been off school for two days according to his eye, which he hurt playing football.

Darren was of school with what I thought was appendersitis but it wasent He was loaded with wind and he hadent been going to the toilet regular the doctor give him medersing to take which give him diharrea But I had my daughter of with spots and the doctror told me to keep her away from other people. Anyway Darren came out in the same spots as his brother did I don't know what they were but I think it was a form of chicken pos spots. Thats why he never returned to school he is better now though.

Jonathan was late for school because 2 gerbils escaped behind the washer.

Rebecca could not come to school today because she has been bothered by very close veins.

Paul was absent on Friday before they broke up because I slept in. Somebody took out the fuse of the main box which is outside the front door and none of us woke up till I looked at my watch at 10.20. Even Lee my youngest son didn't go to school till 12.45 after dinner.

Chris will be absent today and probably tomorrow. As he was walking to school it was snowing and he had his head down and walked into a lamp-post. He has a bruised head.

We had to take Michael to the hospital last night after he fell off his bike and hit his head. Fortunately, when they X-rayed it they found nothing. He will be back tomorrow.

Please excuse Samantha having a shower, being how she is. Being how you are yourself sometimes, you will understand how she is.

Please excuse Josie for being absent yesterday. She was in bed with gramps.

Letter from school to new parents: "At the beginning of each school year we assign pupils to specific lockers. We expect them to remain in the lockers to which they are assigned . . ."

Parents who consider that the behaviour of pupils is unacceptable and uncivil should see the headteacher.

Letter in a Norfolk school magazine . . .

Dear Editor,

I was very distressed to read in your Spring issue a note recording the death of Walter Brown. Of all the Old Boys I knew, he was undoubtedly the one I most admired. I cannot believe he is no longer with us.

Yours sincerely, Walter Brown.

12

Sex

Schools are doing a valiant job in Personal and Social Education in attempting to cultivate in their pupils a sense of responsibility and morality in matters of sexual relationships. It is a task avoided by so many parents who, quite rightly, wish their offspring to be virtuous and decorous while being unwilling or unable to inform them themselves. Unable, perhaps, is the operative word if this letter is anything to go by.

Why all this fuss about sex education in schools? I am sixteen and I taught my mother about reproduction, using the correct biological terms. The present generation of parents cannot tell their children how they came to be born because they do not know. *(Letter in Daily Mirror)*

Perhaps the following observer thought schools should get down to the fundamentals in the Creative Design module . . .

"Too often biology is used in schools as a vehicle for sex education," declared Dr Gilbert Russell, Education Secretary of the Church of England Moral Welfare Council, in Bristol yesterday. *(Western Daily Press and Bristol Mirror)*

Shocking sight

I must add my voice to those who object to the naked bathers on the eastern section of Eastney beach.

Walking with my five-year-old granddaughter I was quite shocked at, and needless to say un-prepared for, the sight of naked male bodies sprawled across the shingle.

Quite obviously, they delighted in showing off their private parts and, my granddaughter being of an impressionable age, I had to tell her these men were fishing with special rods.

It is surely about time the police made a concerted effort to rid this beautiful part of the south coast of these wanton exhibitionists.

Mengham Road
Hayling Island

(The News, Southampton)

And perhaps schools are not always blessed with suitable teachers of the subject . . .

A schoolmistress said at Ilford County Court last Wednesday that she did not like seeing men's short underwear on a clothes-line, and also objected to seeing men's pyjamas hanging in an "indiscreet" way on the line. It caused her embarrassment to see them. *(Ilford Guardian)*

And not everybody benefits from school-based explanations . . .

Mike Harding once said: "When I was at school, the books on sex gave me a terrible inferiority complex."

But these textbooks could have interesting additions . . .

Graffiti – next to heading "SEX APPEAL" was written "Please give generously"!

And certainly the need for sex education is there, judging from the following . . .

A student undergoing a word-association test was asked why a snowstorm put him in mind of sex. He replied frankly: "Because everything does."

A teacher at a school in Buckinghamshire asked which of the senior boys would like to be present at the birth of any children they might have after they were married. One would not commit himself. Pressed for his opinion, he finally said: "Well, Miss, it depends if I know the girl very well."

Q: How important are elections to a democratic society?
A: Sex can only happen when a male gets an election.

And you must always be careful what you say and what you write . . .

A biology teacher was handing out sheets to a Year 11 class on sexual reproduction and enquired: "Right – has anyone still not got their 'Male Reproductive Organs'?"

Humans need to reproduce to continue the specious.

The pill is easy to use and very useful for an eager woman.

Q: From what may men in their fifties suffer?
A: The manopause.

Q: State one change in boys at puberty.
A: Their vice deepens.

Male mammals have eternal sexual organs.

My sister's expecting a baby, and I don't know if I'm going to be an uncle or an aunt.

My father told me all about the birds and the bees. The liar – I went steady with a woodpecker till I was twenty-one. *(Bob Hope)*

I got this black eye fighting for my girlfriend's honour. She would insist on keeping it.

Anne Boleyn: Not tonight, darling. I've got a headache.
Henry VIII: We'll soon fix that!

Boys and girls develop in different places.

Twins are two things which come together unexpectedly.

He had been eating tomatoes and drinking milk, and the woman may have mistaken this as an offer of sex. It was not, he said. *(Rhodesia Herald)*

A sex line caller complained to Trading Standards. After dialling an 0891 number from an advertisement entitled "Hear Me Moan", the caller was played a tape of a woman nagging her husband for failing to do jobs around the house. Consumer Watchdogs in Dorset refused to look into the complaint, saying: "He got what he deserved." *(Gloucester Citizen)*

Police arrived quickly, to find Mr Melchett hanging by his fingertips from the back wall. He had run out of the house when the owner, Paul Finch, returned home unexpectedly and, spotting an intruder in the garden, had dialled 999. What Mr Finch did not know was that Mr Melchett had been visiting Mrs Finch and, hearing the front door open, had climbed out of the rear window. But the back wall was 8 feet high and Mr Melchett had been unable to get his leg over. *(Barnsley Chronicle)*

The money will not be going directly into the prostitutes' pockets, but will be used to encourage them to lead a better life. We will be training them for new positions in hotels. *(Daily Telegraph)*

Police called to arrest a naked man on the platform at Piccadilly Station released their suspect after he produced a valid rail ticket. *(Manchester Evening News)*

For seven and a half years I've worked alongside President Reagan. We've had triumphs. Made some mistakes. We've had some sex . . . uh . . . setbacks. *(George Bush)*

In her statement the girl said that he had put his hand on her chest and a guinea pig which she had under her jumper had bitten him. *(Cannock Advertiser)*

It is comforting to know that our MPs are trying to instil a bit of morality . . .

BRAZIER'S ANGER AT SEX TOYS

MP Julian Brazier is getting hot under the collar about a scheme to issue sex aid at Family Planning Clinics across the Country. The Chairman of the Conservative Family Campaign is angry that vibrators are being handed out willy nilly on the National Health. *(Canterbury Times)*

But in America . . .

Walter Mondale: George Bush doesn't have the manhood to apologize.
Bush: Well, on the manhood thing, I'll put mine up against his any time.

13

Parents

It is amazing how much the body figures, in some shape or form, with parents.

7th August 1915: On the bus the other day a woman with a baby sat opposite, the baby bawled, and the woman at once began to unlace herself, exposing a large, red bosom, which she swung into the baby's face. The infant, however, continued to cry and the woman said: "Come on now, there's a good boy – if you don't I shall give it to the gentleman opposite." *(The Journal of a Disappointed Man, W.N.P. Barbellion)*

And on the same theme . . .

Stockport Research Interest Group. Wednesday, January 28, 7pm, School of Nursing. Stepping Hill Hospital. Speaker Anne Thompson: "Why don't women breast feed? Cheese and wine party follows."

At an annual dinner for parents, a woman eventually turned to the gentleman next to her who had not stopped talking all evening and said: "The story of your pelvis has fascinated me throughout dinner, but I think I should point out that I am a Doctor of Chemistry."

The mother had always said, whenever any of her three children received a knock on the head or knee, "Gentle, gentle, it will be all right." As a result knocks in the family become known as "gentles". One day Dad had fallen from a step ladder, landed on his knees and skinned them. The next day as he sat waiting in a crowded shopping centre for the family, the four-year-old ran up and jumped on his knee, in the process catching his injured knee-caps. As he winced, audibly and visibly, the little girl shouted back to her mother: "Oh dear, Mammy, I think I've hurt Daddy's 'gentles'." Passers-by were greatly amused.

My husband and I had just put our children to bed when we heard sobbing coming from three-year-old Eric's room. Rushing to his side, we found that he had accidentally swallowed a penny and was sure he was going to die.

Desperate to calm him down, my husband palmed a penny from his pocket and pretended to pull it from Eric's ear. Eric was delighted. He snatched the coin from my husband's hand, swallowed it and demanded cheerfully: "Go on, Dad – do it again!"

There are the proud parents . . .

Comment by proud mother at a parents' consultation evening: "I keep telling him – if he sticks in and gets these GCSEs, then the world's his lobster."

Two mothers were talking about a recent fancy dress party outside a primary school in Leeds:
Q: Did your little daughter enjoy herself?
A: Oh, yes, she looked lovely. We dressed her up in one of those Japanese commodes.

"Alan broke his leg in two places a month ago at nursery school – we don't know how!" his father laughed. *(Slough Observer)*

There are the troublesome . . .

Dad volunteered to babysit one night so Mum could have an evening out. At bedtime, he sent the youngsters upstairs to bed and settled down to read the newspapers. One child kept creeping down the stairs, but Dad kept sending him back. At 9.00 pm the doorbell rang. It was the next door neighbour, Mrs Smith, asking whether her son was there. The father brusquely replied: "No". Just then a little head appeared over the bannister and a voice shouted: "I'm here, Mam, but he won't let me go home."

At the court hearing following the junior school football match, the mother said she was not very abusive, but she did call Mr — "a monkey-faced, button-eyed old g-t". *(Liverpool Echo)*

You really do no good by constantly scalding a child. *(Women's magazine)*

Headteacher: I am very sorry that your son was picked upon and punched in the ordeal.
Mother: He wasn't. He was punched right in the stomach and kicked where it hurts.

Parental expressions every child should know even though they only lead to irritability and resentment . . .

Some day you'll thank me.
I don't want to hear any more about it.
When I was your age . . .
You don't know when you are well off.

We had to eat what we were given.
We would never have dared say that to our parents.
We had to be in by nine o'clock.
I wish that I had had the opportunities you have.
We had to be happy with two days at Blackpool for our holidays.
We were happy with a tangerine and a few nuts for Christmas.
As long as you live in my house . . .
How many times have I told you . . .?
This is hurting me more than it's hurting you - apropos of which reassurance . . .

Father, chancing to chastise
His indignant daughter Sue,
Said: "I hope you realise
That this hurts me more than you."
Susan ceased to roar;
"If that's really true," said she,
"I can stand a good deal more;
Pray go on, and don't mind me."
(Harry Graham, Ruthless Rhymes 1899)

Children can be equally irritable when they come out with such bons mots to parents as . . .

This is the 1990s, you know!
Times have changed since the First World War.
All my friends can . . ./have . . .

Parental odds and ends . . .

I have found that the best way to give advice to your children is to find out what they want and then advise them to do it. *(Harry S. Truman)*

Doctor: I don't like the look of your husband.
Wife: I don't, either, but he's good to the children.

Parent: John hasn't arrived back home.
Headteacher: Didn't he tell you? He's gone to see *Dr Zhivago* today.
Parent: What's the matter with him now, then?

Mother: Did you enjoy your visit to the zoo with Daddy today?
Eight-year-old: Yes and so did Daddy – especially when one of the animals came in at 20-1.

A teacher asked her class of eight-year-olds to write about their personal heroes. One little girl brought her essay home and showed it to her parents. Her father was flattered to discover that his daughter had chosen him. "Why did you pick me?" he asked expectantly. "Because I couldn't spell 'Schwarzenegger,'" the little girl replied.

14

Newspapers

MAGGIE SOLD! An autographed photo of Margaret Thatcher fetched £1.60 at a school auction sale in Oyne, Aberdeenshire. A box of haddock raised £8. *(Sunday Mail)*

CORRECTION – Due to a printing error, a story in last week's *Gazette* referred to school athletics coach Billy Hodgkins as an "old waster". This should, of course, have read "old master". We apologise to Mr Hodgkins for any embarrassment this has caused.

A talk on guide dogs for the blind will be given at Brazeley Library, Cedar Avenue, Horwich, on Monday at 7.30 pm The talk will be given by Mrs Wooff. *(Bolton Journal)*

But Alderman Rita Ubriaco criticized the motion, saying the objection was similar to a recent action by the nearby Dryden Board of Education ". . . who damned *Lord of the Flies* because they thought it had to do with men's trousers." *(Montreal Gazette)*

(Pictured left) 17-year-old Lynda Stuart from Barbados, photographed at home in Cobham with her pet dog, who has been chosen as head pupil of Westminster School. *(The Lady)*

Museums enable people to explore collections for inspiration, learing and enjoyment. *(British Association of Friends of Museums newsletter)*

Owing to a transcription error, an article in Saturday's *Independent* on page 9 on Irish premier Charles Haughey mistakenly read "A man of immense rudeness". This was intended to read "A man of great shrewdness". *(Independent)*

Dudley's Head of Schools said: "Last month we had a special in-service course on bullying for members of school staffs." *(County Express, Stourbridge)*

Written around the edge of my son's "I am 2" badge taken from a birthday card are the words "Unsuitable for children under 3 years of age". *(Jane Fallows, Gordonvale, Queensland)*

Redbridge Borough Council is to prosecute a school in its district after its kitchens were found to be overrun with cockroaches. The Council decided to take action when the cockroaches were still found in the kitchens three weeks after they had received a warning. *(Grauniad)*

Academy-award-winning documentary in which Jacques d'Amboise, principal dancer of the New York City Ballet, leads a thousand children in his annual gaga performance. *(Bradford Telegraph and Argus)*

There are also the universities, in which it is estimated that one person in 1150 is educated. *(Northumberland newspaper)*

The current *Radio Times* has an interview about exams with John Mann, secretary of the Schools Council, which quotes him as saying: "It is not very satisfactory to divide kids into sheep and goats . . ."

A remittance prince? While the British press speculates that **Prince Andrew** is being sent to Lakefield College School to help Canada through a constitutional crisis, our sources tell us that the real reaxon for the prince's being sent to Cannadda in midterm is that heb xng bi& ng $!((prondi iic454- % BNOThb;t cppty whhhhhhenn e9090 ()() whch isssn't too sprising to those who know the boy's private interests. *(Toronto Sun)*

An urgent investigation has been launched by Solihull Council after a local schoolgirl was involved in a freak accident this week. Keeley Carter, aged 11, fell from stairs at Kinghurst Junior School, North Solihull, impaling her mouth on a 6ft wooden steak, at Monday lunchtime. *(Solihull News)*

Extra money for spending on schools means that no child in a York school needs to go outside to the toilet. In some cases after waiting for nearly 100 years! Phew – that's a relief. *(Labour Party leaflet)*

Football Club helps stab tragedy children
(Northern Echo)

- **LABOUR ROSE**

NEWS FROM THE CITY OF
YORK LABOUR PARTY

THOUGHT FOR TODAY: The whle wrod is in a state of chassis – Sean O'Casey *(The Rising Nepal)*

Madam – I am writing in response to the article on last week's front page of the *Standard* about proposals for a professional creche facility to be launched in the old hospital records office and cottages. As a parent of teenagers I am very aware and concerned about the needs of gangsters in the town at present. From the mid to late teens there is nowhere for them to go in the evenings as a drop-in facility other than pubs. *(Wilts & Glos. Standard)*

All the children in the picture were born after Mrs — and her husband parted in 1930. Altogether she has had eighteen children – fourteen of them, she says, by various fathers. Mrs — says: "It has been a hard job bringing them up. But I am proud of my family. I neither smoke nor go to the cinema. My only relaxation is the radio." *(Sunday Pictorial)*

A bovine bingo game is being staged on the school playing fields on Sunday. A cow will be brought to the field, and where she makes her first deposit will be the lucky spot. The winner gets 25 per cent of the proceeds up to £100, and lots of pats on the back. *(St Albans Review & Express)*

Names of town, district council chairmen and their vices released *(Malawi Daily Times)*

A school spokesman said: "He will be sorely missed at the Rectory, most of all perhaps for his wife's counsel and considerate nature, for which countless staff, parents and pupils had cause to be grateful." *(Richmond and Twickenham Star)*

Much-travelled Royal Marine: Since leaving Cottage Grove (St Luke's) School, in 1942, Sergeant James Robert Newman (49) considers he has had a full and exciting wife. *(Hants Telegraph)*

Emma Duncan, of Lancaster Girls' Grammar School, passed four A-Levels in her recent exams, not ½ as was printed last week. *(S. Blyth, Cumberland News)*

What is dyselxia? *(Nursery World)*

Meetings

● DYSLEXIA: Occupational Therapist at Alder Hey Hospital Wendy Smith will be addressing the Liverpool Dyselxia Association on Wednesday at Liverpool Hope University College.

(Liverpool Echo)

An interesting address on "The National Care of the Child" by Miss Palmer was much appreciated by all, and Mrs Lever in a short address made an appeal for the use of the humane killer. *(Berkshire newspaper)*

In last week's notebook under the heading "What's in a name?" the name of a Honolulu councillor was misspelt as Mr Kekoalaulionapalihauliulio David Kaapuawaokamehaheha. This should have read: Mr

Kekoalauliionapalihauliulio David Kaapuawaokame-haheha. *(Municipal Journal)*

The tutors also complain of the many sixth-form candidates who appear at interviews in open-neck shirts and whose aplications fomrs abound in spelling mistake. *(Daily Telegraph)*

The parents say they are not concerned with the rights and wrongs of the teachers' dispute – only with the welfare of the chicken. *(Newcastle Evening Chronicle)*

The Misses Doris, Agnes and Vivian Smith are spending several days at the home of their mother, Mrs W.L. Lawrence. This is the first time that the community has had the pleasure of seeing the Smith girls in the altogether at one time. *(Sydney Daily News)*

He is the son of the ancient principal of our college who, behind his thick glasses, hid a heart of gold. *(Courrier de Saône et Loire)*

Embarrassed BBC Television officials admitted last night that their exclusive film of the Loch Ness Monster was, in fact, a duck. *(Daily Telegraph)*

DID YOU KNOW . . .? The first Boy Scout troop in Vermont was organised in Vermont. *(Middlebury Independent)*

Daventry Development Committee are looking for two pretty girls to show off their expansion regions. *(Northampton Chronicle and Echo)*

Crash courses are available for those wishing to learn to drive very quickly. *(Eastbourne Gazette)*

A colleague was tuned to a provincial radio station. The disc jockey introduced a record for a listener "who's 111 today". *[Pause]* "Sorry. That's not 111. He's ill."

Once again I felt that there is no more creative and health-giving activity for the young than the preservation, resuscitation and running of a railway worked by steam locomotives. *(Letter from the Master of a Cambridge college in The Times)*

In our report last week of Davison School PTA Fête we referred to Mr Ron Marshall as being the late organiser. This should have read fête organiser. We apologise for the error. *(Worthing Gazette)*

FULLY FURNISHED HOUSE – 3 kitchens, 2 bathrooms, 3 toilets. Suitable students. £30 per student per wee. *(Express and Echo, Exeter)*

If they could save children from dying before the age of one, there would be a better prospect of them reaching to adolescence. *(South London newspaper)*

LUCKY CARETAKER
WAS STABBED THREE TIMES

PUPILS CUT
TO EASE CROWDING

. . . and the second seminar will be on the unorganised conference . . . er . . . I'm sorry – the UN organised conference.

The computer class for nudists, 50-strong, consists of housewives, teachers, doctors, engineers and office workers. Dr R. J. Gibson, club secretary, explained that it is being started partly because the weather is not always suitable for badminton. *(Sunday Citizen)*

Sandhurst captain-coach Ron Best made it 105 girls for the season yesterday, when he booted 13 goals against Kennington. *(Bendigo Advertiser, Australia)*

A foreign teacher nicknamed "Mr Wortical", who was sacked from a primary school because his spoken English and grammar were said to be below standard, had been adjudged "not goon enough to teach in primary schools" before he took the post, it was revealed yesterday. *(Daily Telegraph)*

The birth rate declined, in the period 1972-1978, from 20.82 per thousand people to 15.98. A main cause of all this is the difficulty of making ends meet. *(Observer)*

All he asked was a fireside chair and a couple of good boobs. *(Cape Times)*

Presbyterian crossing facilities outside the school have been championed by the councillor.

The production at St Clare's was beautifully moved and staged. Gropings were splendid and moves were well thought out.

Sister Gillian's "bust clinic" referred to last month was, of course, a "busy clinic".

The annual Christmas party at the Ashley Street School was hell yesterday afternoon. *(Springfield newspaper)*

I know Sir Peter Parker hasn't forgotten me. I remember him at the dancing class as a girl of 14. *(London Evening Standard)*

The shooting of the cadet force was excellent. The shooting of the sergeant major was especially satisfactory. *(Daily Express)*

John Harkes going to Sheffield, Wednesday. *(New York Post)*

9pm Broadcast on behalf of the Conservative Party. 10pm They Think It's All Over. *(Independent)*

Water levels are low. Why not fill up the reservoirs from the mains? *(Letter in the Poole Daily Echo)*

The age limit for Girl Guides was formerly 18 years, but now by general request it has now been raised to 81 years. *(Local newspaper)*

WOMAN HURT WHILE COOKING HER HUSBAND'S BREAKFAST IN A HORRIBLE MANNER *(Texas newspaper)*

The little children are more outgoing than the adults. They have all made genuine friends here and we have no problems at all – well, only one. The smallest were not used to wearing knickers. *(Daily Telegraph)*

Princess — on her way to school. She attends a co-educational establishment at which are a number of other children. *(Daily Telegraph)*

We apologise for the error in last week's paper in which we stated that Mr Arnold Dogbody was a defective in the police force. This was a typographical error. We meant, of course, that Mr Dogbody is a detective in the police farce and we are sorry for any embarrassment caused. *(Ely Standard)*

The British legal system is the best in the World. Each case is tried with scrupulous fairness and justice is not only done, it is seen to be done. There are no inflexible rules: the law is elastic. *(US college magazine)*

Overcome by gas while taking a shower, she owed her life to the watchfulness of the caretaker. *(Cheshire Weekly)*

MISS FRIAN, FORMER PRINCIPAL, UNVEILS BUST AT DEDICATION CEREMONY *(Catchgate College magazine)*

The Mayor was visiting the school with his bitter half. *(Consett Times)*

Widower, 50s, teacher, C of E, own home, wishes to meet

widow for fiendship. *(Express and Star, Wolverhampton)*

The report was signed by five faulty members of the University. *(Herald & Post)*

Mr Okum, the chairman of Governors, lives with his wife, his childhood sweetheart, and three sons in Chalmonte. *(Bury Advertiser)*

The all-girl orchestra were rather weak in the bras section. *(Slough Times)*

A village teacher in Spain turned his horse upside down in a frantic search for a missing lottery ticket while villagers waited outside for news. *(Daily Telegraph)*

She is now a language teacher but was a former dental nurse of Finnish extraction. *(Mail on Sunday)*

I took my eight-year-old to the Doctor, a Dutchman, when she had flu. He asked her how she felt. "I'm all clogged up," she replied. *(Letter in Durham Advertiser)*

During the school match, Meads was kicked on the head, and had to have three stitches put in the cut. Kirkpatrick broke his nose early in the match. Villepreux played most of the game with two ribs broken. Many others were hurt. Some of the injuries were deliberately inflicted. These deeds made unpleasant watching. But, taken as a whole, this was not a game that got out of hand. *(Guardian)*

The thirteen pupils were able to see the hospital's special baby car unit. *(Thurrock Gazette)*

HORSE GIRL SUSPENDED BY HEAD *(Daily Telegraph)*

It was decided in the redevelopment that, at the centre of the college, Copcastle Square would be made into a rotunda with a doomed roof. *(Bury Evening Telegraph)*

IRAQI HEAD SEEKS ARMS *(Newspaper headline)*

(Needham Market newsletter)

Spoken Bloopers

The king of verbal cock-ups was Murray Walker as he commentated animatedly and sometimes hysterically through the microphone. Clive James described him thus: 'Murray sounds like a blindfolded man riding a unicycle on the rim of the pit of doom,' adding, 'Even in moments of tranquillity, Murray Walker sounds like a man whose trousers are on fire.' Some of his more hilarious remarks can serve as an introduction to this section . . .

Jensen Button is in the top ten, in eleventh position.

And he's lost both right front tyres.

Mansell can see him in his earphone.

Do my eyes deceive me, or is Senna's Lotus sounding rough?

I know it's a cliché, but you can cut the atmosphere with a cricket bat.

Tambay's hopes, which were nil before, are absolutely zero now.

This has been a great season for Nelson Piquet, as he is now known, and always has been.

And Damon Hill is following . . . Damon Hill.

Jean Alesi is fourth and fifth.

Mansell is slowing down taking it easy. Oh, no he isn't! It's a lap record.

It's lap 26 of 58, which unless I'm very much mistaken is half way.

I was there when I said it.

Of course, he did it voluntarily, but he had to.

Others, besides Murray, became well known for putting their feet in it, and some are worthy of mention, particularly former US Vice President Dan Quayle . . .

If we do not succeed then we run the risk of failure.

I deserve respect for the things I did not do.

The President is leading us out of this recovery.

The US victory in the Gulf War was a stirring victory for the forces of aggression.

The loss of life will be irreplaceable.

And then there are others . . .

Rarely is the question asked: 'Is our children learning?' *(George Bush)*

A zebra does change its spots. *(Al Gore)*

Let's give the terrorists a fair trial and then hang them. *(Senator Gary Hart)*

You can argue about that until the cows come home. *(Environment Minister Elliot Morley in radio debate during foot and mouth outbreak)*

The best cure for insomnia is to get a lot of sleep. *(Senator Hyakawa)*

. . . the wind is shining, and the sun is blowing gently across the fields. *(Ray Laurence)*

I asked the barmaid for a quickie. I was mortified when the man next door to me said, 'It's pronounced "quiche".' *(Italian Ambassador Luigi Amaduzzi)*

An end is in sight to the severe weather shortage. *(Ian McCaskill)*

They couldn't hit an elephant from this dist–. *(Last words of General Segwick in the American Civil War*

Why only twelve disciples? Go out and get thousands. *(Sam Goldwyn)*

Let us toast the queer old Dean. *(Rev. W.A. Spooner)*

Sir, you have tasted two whole worms. *(Rev. W.A. Spooner)*

You will leave Oxford on the next town drain. *(Rev. W.A. Spooner)*

Gaffes and the media

Unless the teachers receive a higher salary increase they

may decide to leave their pests. *(Times Educational Supplement)*

Some of the boys' methods are quite ingenious, the professors at the Institute have found. For instance, when asked to multiply 20 by 24 mentally, one gave the answer – 600 – in a few seconds. *(Baltimore Sun)*

It's ten o'clock, Greenwich. Meantime, here is the news. *(Heard on the radio)*

Here's Miller running in to bowl. He's got two short legs and one behind. *(Cricket commentator)*

He's got a great future ahead. But he's missed so much of it. *(Terry Venables)*

And tonight Northern areas can expect incest and rain – er, sorry about that, incessant rain. *(Radio weather presenter)*

Remember the name – it's big Seven and U-P after.' *(Radio advert)*

Fiona May only lost out on the gold medal because Niurka Montalvo jumped further than she did. *(David Coleman)*

Do you believe David Trimble will stick to his guns on decommissioning? *(Radio One Newsbeat)*

It was the fastest-ever swim over that distance on American soil. *(Interviewer, UTV)*

Despite fears that the balloon may be forced to ditch in the Pacific, Mr Branson remains buoyant and hopes to reach America. *(Portsmouth News)*

It has been the German Army's largest peacetime operation since World War 2. *(Radio 5 Live)*

Do Britain's drug laws need a shot in the arm? *(CNN News)*

Police and Customs officers retrieved a cannabis haul today in a joint operation. *(Radio Cleveland)*

Ian Mackie is here to prove his back injury is behind him. *(Radio 4)*

And that was played by the Lindsay String Quartet . . . or, at least, two thirds of them. *(Template Times)*

Headlines with a difference

THE LIFE OF HORATIO NELSON – For details see top of column *(Radio Times)*

MAD COW TALKS *(Huddersfield Daily Examiner)*

NOTHING SUCKS LIKE AN ELECTROLUX *(Used by the Scandinavian vacuum manufacturer in an American advertising campaign)*

COUNCIL STAMPS ON DOG'S MESS *(Leighton Observer)*

SURVIVOR OF SIAMESE TWINS JOINS PARENTS *(Boston Globe)*

IRAQ HEAD SEEKS ARMS *(Sydney Mercury)*

EYE DROPS OFF SHELF *(Medical News Magazine)*

JUVENILE COURT TO TRY SHOOTING DEFENDANT *(Court News)*

STOLEN PAINTING FOUND BY TREE *(Slalom Post)*

TWO SISTERS RE-UNITED AFTER 18 YEARS ON CHECK-OUT COUNTER *(Financial Mail)*

RESIDENTS FLEA IN ARSON ATTACK *(Worthing Herald)*

CARLESS DRIVING CASE IS ADJOURNED *(Scarborough Evening News)*

PROSTITUTES APPEAL TO THE POPE

COUPLE SLAIN. POLICE SUSPECT HOMICIDE

CONMEN PRAYING ON VULNERABLE PEOPLE

PANDA MATING FAILS: VET TAKES OVER

ASTRONAUT TAKES BLAME FOR GAS IN SPACE

KIDS MAKE NUTRITIOUS SNACKS

SOMETHING WENT WRONG IN JET CRASH

COLD WAVE LINKED TO TEMPERATURES

LOCAL HIGH SCHOOL DROPOUTS CUT IN HALF

TYPHOON RIPS THROUGH CEMETERY – THOUSANDS

DEAD

TWO SOVIET SHIPS COLLIDE – ONE DIES

LUNG CANCER IN WOMEN MUSHROOMS

SCHOOLBUS PASSENGERS SHOULD HAVE BEEN BELTED

POLICE CAMPAIGN TO RUN DOWN JAY-WALKERS

TROOPS WATCH ORANGE MARCH

CHEF THROWS HEART INTO FEEDING NEEDY FAMILIES

BRITISH UNION FINDS DWARFS (sic) IN SHORT SUPPLY

POLICE SUBDUED MAN WITH CARVING KNIFE

STEALS CLOCK, FACES TIME

PASSENGERS HIT BY CANCELLED TRAINS

POLICE FOUND DRUNK IN SHOP WINDOW

NEW SHOCKS ON ELECTRICITY BILLS

POLICE SAY DETECTIVE SHOT MAN WITH KNIFE

PRESSMEN GATHER TO SEE ROYALS HUNG AT WINDSOR

CATERING COLLEGE HEAD COOKED FOR THE QUEEN

MAN IN THAMES HAD A DRINK PROBLEM

COUNCIL DECIDE TO MAKE SAFE DANGER SPOTS

FIREMEN TO SHOW THEIR APPLIANCES TO PASSERS-BY TO ATTRACT RECRUITS

CHAMBERMAID HAD POT

FARMER'S EIGHT-HOUR VIGIL IN BOG

PEER'S SEAT BURNS ALL NIGHT – ANCIENT PILE DESTROYED

SAVAGE APPOINTED HIGH COURT JUDGE

SHELL FOUND ON BEACH

FILMING IN CEMETERY ANGERS RESIDENTS

NO WATER – SO FIREMEN IMPROVISED

PRISONERS ESCAPE AFTER EXECUTION

ANTIQUE DEALER THOUGHT GIRL WAS OLDER

GAS RIG MEN GRILLED BY VILLAGERS

STAR'S BROKEN LEG HITS BOX OFFICE

QUEEN SEES FONTEYN TAKE 10 CURTAINS

SPOTTED MAN WANTED FOR QUESTIONING

SPARE OUR TREES – THEY BREAK WIND

And getting it right below the headlines can be a tricky business, too!

On making enquiries at the hospital this afternoon, we learn that the deceased is as well as can be expected. *(Jersey Evening Post)*

A woman mourner was horrified when her best hat was buried with the coffin at a South African funeral – she had planned to wear it to a cocktail party later the same day but an undertaker mistook it for a floral tribute. *(Weekend)*

The bride was attended by two bridesmaids. Both were nearly attired in dresses of fawn georgette. *(Lincolnshire paper)*

The landlord insisted that no female should be allowed in the bra without a man. *(Glasgow Herald)*

ROY ROGERS – Roy Rogers, 66, singing cowboy star of many films and television westerns, was in a 'stable condition' yesterday after undergoing open-heart surgery at Torrance, near Los Angeles. *(Daily Telegraph)*

Bulmers achieved its position after a programme to improve conditions for its 1,000-strong Hereford workforce, which have included profit-sharing, annual bonuses and a 35-day week. *(Hereford News)*

Responsible preventative measures such as neutering need to be taken very seriously by car owners. *(York Evening Press)*

The Canine Defence League also offers a low cost neutering service to pensioners and people on means-tested benefits.

(West Briton)

Have you got the longest legs in the East Midlands? Pretty Polly has announced that gorgeous and glamorous Tania Strecker is the new face of Pretty Polly Nylons, modelling its recently re-launched bestselling hosiery range with her amazing 37 legs. *(Long Eaton Trader)*

Correction: Hakin girl wins lap dancing certificate. The headline should have read: Hakin girl wins tap dancing certificate.
(Milford & West Wales Mercury)

Many people were dubious about the prospect of a large metal deer in the park, fearing it could turn into a white elephant. *(Ealing Gazette)*

The Institute Management Committee held its monthly meeting in the committee room. Alan Day, chairman, showed samples of carpet, which will be used in the ladies toilets and carried through the reading rooms. *(Westmorland Gazette)*

Brigadier Chris Sextor unveiled the plague with officials. *(KM Extra)*

The toilets were in a terrible state, they hadn't had a penny spent on them since the sixties. *(Manchester Metro News)*

The Women's Institute will hold their fortnightly lecture in St Mary's Hall, the topic will be 'Country Life' when Mrs Wills will show slides of some beautiful wild pants. *(Matlock Mercury)*

Personally, I would welcome a plague dedicated to Bill

Owen because he was a fine actor . . . *(Huddersfield Daily Examiner)*

At a meeting to discuss the route of a proposed ring road, the highways committee chairman said: 'We intend to take the road through the cemetery – provided we can get permission from the various bodies concerned.' *(West London Observer)*

I was so pleased to read that the city councillors rejected plans to turn Worcester Angel Mall into a café brassiere. *(Worcester Evening News)*

15

Adverts

Significant mis-spellings can make a major difference . . .

From *The Times Educational Supplement* . . .

APPOINTMENT OF
FIRST
HEADMASTER
THE INGLISH SCHOOL—ESTEPONA
An Educational Cooperative and Trust
(approved by the Spanish Government)
Estepona (Malaga), Spain

And from the *South China Morning Post* . . .

GREAT YARMOUTH OPEN BOWELS FESTIVAL –
Great Yarmouth Bowling Greens, Marine Parade
(What's On, When and Where – East Anglia)

Teachers – Why not Explore France on a Horse? – Village
Gits, Self Catering or Full Board *(Horse & Pony)*

Wendy House – suitable for 3-4 year-old. Good condition –
very turdy *(Evening Gazette)*

Technician Required For De Brus School . . . Good
interpersonal and communicatino skills would be an
advantage.

Garden refuge collected.

And if they really meant what they said . . .

Advert in the Western Gazette . . .

FRIENDS' ACADEMY, Locust Valley, Long Island, Co-
educational, with special opportunities for boys. *(Friend's
Intelligencer)*

The Indian Express is proud to announce . . .

Artificial Limbs Centre has new head
Express News Service

And a good camping opportunity in Southport . . .

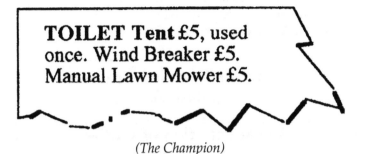

TOILET Tent £5, used once. Wind Breaker £5. Manual Lawn Mower £5.

(The Champion)

While Camera Weekly issues an unusual invitation . . .

74 Diary: where to shoot kids singing carols in a courtyard and the best guide to photogenic country walks

. . . and as for the *Korean Weekly* **. . . !**

대영여행사

Dai Young Travel

Dialectical Materialist and elderly mother require housekeeper. *(Daily Worker)*

THREE GIRLS, navy school skirts, age 11 years. £10 the lot. *(Lancaster Grauniad)*

10.50 [FILM] LAP DANCER (Arthur Egell, 1995) Erotic drama – starring Elizabeth Wagner as a woman who turns to lap dancing to make ends meet. *89578976*
12.15 NFL American Football

Children's Branded Trainers
(adidas)

Large selection of Ladies aerobic wear
(adidas/puma)

Children's Branded Bottoms from £12

(Ukay Clothing – Norfolk Citizen)

NORTHWOOD PREPARATORY SCHOOL (MOOR PARK) – LUNCHTIME PLAY SUPERVISOR for our 408 year old boys. Please tel. Mrs Hampel on . . .

TYPING * SHORTHAND * AUDIO-TYPING. Learn with a qualified tutor. Morning sessions 9.15am-12.15pm. Beginners, refreshers or nature students. *(Whitstable Extra)*

THE HITE REPORT ON MALE SEXUALITY (September: £12 [cased]; £9.95 [limp])

*Advert from **The Times Educational Supplement** . . .*

Wanted Head of Junior School . . . Roll is largely Muslim. Strong Church of England links and a regular communicant preferred.

Our FREE teachers' educational package is very suggestive indeed. *(Advertising flyer for canal boat trips around Birmingham)*

And then there are the courses on offer . . .

Girls and Boys in School – The course is intended for headmasters, deputy headmasters and other staff. *(Details of equal opportunities course offered under the Council of Europe teacher bursary scheme)*

Exams. Learn the principles of success in studying and passing exams. One day course. *(Wirral Globe)*

South Glamorgan Institute for Higher Education, Cardiff, is offering Degree in Dietetics (four-year Sandwich Course).

BEBE CAR DUPLA TANDEM PRAM and all accessories £150, Britax Rocker Bye £15, plus Walker £15, and baby £5. *(Herald and Post)*

Six Faces of Wine
CHALFONT'S COUNTY SECONDARY SCHOOL
NICOL ROAD. Weds 7.45–9.15pm 6 fortnightly
meetings 12 January 1983. Ms P Drinkwater

Spotted in Buckinghamshire WEA Brochure . . .

Rentokil Pest Control Division wish St Theresa's Prep School another 40 pest-free years. *(The Universe)*

NORTHFIELD GARDEN PARTY – 17 JULY, 2.00-5.00. STALLS – GAMES – MUSIC – COMPETITIONS. NB Bring an umbrella! No toilet facilities provided.

BURROWS BOOKSHOP – Visit us for a wide choice of Summer reading. Holiday and Leisure Guides. Children's books to keep them abused in the holidays, and lots, lots more. *(The Ely Crier)*

Extract from the South China Morning Post . . .

From the program of a forthcoming Royal College of Physicians' conference on the medical effects of alcohol:

    9.20:   Effects of alcohol on the heart
    9.50:   Alcohol and the heart
    10.20: Alcohol and the nervous system
    11.20: Effects of alcohol on the
              gastrointestinal system
    10.10: Nutrition and alcohol
    12.40: Bar open

Intelligent young European lady wanted for interesting and responsible work. Typing useful but not essential.

PULL-OUT
Exam tables in full

Analysis
SECTION 1
Pages 4,5

Must be proper good at grammer and spelling. *(Handscodt Bugle and Advertiser)*

Sign in School Cafeteria in Worcester: "Shoes are required to eat in the cafeteria." Underneath was written: "Socks can eat wherever they want."

16

Notices

Notices, which in recent years have proliferated almost as much as circulars, and intrude upon our lives from street to stretcher, frequently give conflicting messages . . .

ANY PERSON NOT PUTTING LITTER INTO THIS BASKET WILL BE LIABLE TO A FINE OF £5 *(But, Sir, I haven't got any litter!)*

DOGS MUST BE CARRIED ON THE ESCALATORS *(And what if I don't have a dog?)*

SCHOOL OF THE SISTERS OF CHARITY *– NO PARKING – NO TURNING*

PLEASE DO NOT LOCK THE DOOR AS WE HAVE LOST THE KEY

Please do not feed the ducks. If you have any suitable food, please give it to the teachers on duty.

BELL OUT OF USE – PLEASE USE KNOCKERS

SWIMMING POOL – PEDESTRIANS ONLY

The spare key to the First Aid Room is available in the First Aid Room. *(Sign in Kent school)*

PLEASE TAKE A TRAY *(And what happened when Jimmy tried to walk out the door with one under his arm?)*

CHILDREN FOUND STRAYING WILL BE TAKEN TO THE LION HOUSE *(Notice at Kyo Zoo)*

Year 7 are saving aluminium cans, bottles and other items to be recycled. Proceeds will be used to cripple children.

Assistant Cook Required For St Anselm's Secondary School (No Objection to Sex)

Mrs Kearney would be grateful for anything you want to get rid of for the Christmas fayre on Thursday evening. Why not come and bring your parents?

TOILET OUT OF ORDER. PLEASE USE FLOOR BELOW.

You are invited to take advantage of the chambermaid. *(Japanese hotel)*

Visitors are expected to complain at the office between the hours of 9 and 11 a.m. daily. *(Athens hotel)*

And when a single letter, or phrase, can make such a difference . . .

A seven-pound baby boy arrived last night *to frighten* the lives of Mr and Mrs Caswell.

Congratulations to Alan and his wife Amy on the *girth* of their first child.

The senior choir invites any member of the school who enjoys *signing* to join the choir.

The head will be away for the rest of the week. *Massages* can be given to his secretary.

Mrs Thomas Jennings' classes for children of pre-kindergarten age will be resumed on Mondays, Wednesdays and Fridays, from 9 to 12 o'clock. A slight *smack* will be served at about 10.30. *(Connecticut paper)*

The Low Self Esteem Group will meet Thursday at 12.30 pm. Please use the back door.

Year 9 will be presenting Shakespeare's *Hamlet* in the main hall at 7 pm tonight. All staff are invited to attend this tragedy.

Mr and Mrs John Bowley, both teachers, are the parents of their child, a daughter born at Windsor Hospital on August 15th.

Lost in school yesterday – tan leather wallet, containing photographs, personal cuttings, and £50. Finder may keep photographs, clippings and the wallet, but the owner has a personal attachment to the money.

FOR SALE: an antique desk suitable for lady with thick legs and large drawers.

Notices/Signs/Announcements/Small Ads/Labels

IN CASE OF FIRE, PLEASE DO YOUR UTMOST TO ALARM THE SCHOOL CARETAKER *(School notice)*

The typists' reproduction equipment is not to be interfered with without the prior permisssion of the office manager. *(On school staff-room notice board)*

Staff should empty the teapot and then stand upside down on the tea tray *(Staff-room notice board)*

Afterwards mice pies and wine will be served and anyone wishing to sing a song will be welcome. *(Halifax Evening Courier)*

MEXICAN NIGHT – Complimentary Punch On Arrival *(Promotional flyer)*

Join us in the drawing room for a pre-dinner drink. Pour over the menu and place your order. *(Time-share brochure)*

. . . currently have vacancy for the following: Brassiere Supervisor *(Wigan Reporter)*

Bring Me Sunshine – Male, 55, 5'10'', enjoys bawling, dancing, socialising, seeks female for friendship. *(Northampton Evening Telegraph)*

Genital male, lonely 35, single dad, 5ft 10, dark hair, brown eyes, seeks female, for friendship and romance. *(Towcester Post)*

Experienced Au Pair Girl, experienced in housework. Especially enjoys cooing. *(Evening Standard)*

BOX of mixed body parts, suitable car boot. *(Alton Gazette)*

Retired lady seeks modern gent, 60–70, must be non-smoker with a good sense of humour, honest, loving and reliable, to enjoy each other's company, must be impotent. *(Louth Target)*

Deep freeze meat: best Scotch meat from Wales. *(Edinburgh Evening News)*

1990s LARGE pram, with rain cover, sun canopy and mattress, ideal for grandparents, £20. *(South Wales Evening Post)*

CAN YOU LOSE 15LB BETWEEN NOW AND CHRISTMAS? YES! Natural products, follow-up service. Phone Christ on . . . *(Boston Standard)*

LOST – Lost at the Coigach Gathering, a stainless steel vacuum flask. Used for collecting veterinary faeces samples. May have been mistaken for hot drinks flask. *(Ullapool News)*

(This sign from Plevna, Montana where a letter has fallen off)

Plevna Public school

Are you fit and healthy? Do you enjoy working with people? Yes? Then we need you, FULL or PART TIME. Both positions are on a shit roster.

PART-TIME PEOPLE – required to fill sandwiches.

Please write your name in the log. *(At the entrance to the local sewage works)*

A police crackdown on credit fraud has been given a major boost after a detective forged vital links with American banks. *(Kentish Times)*

NESTING BIRDS – YOU MUST NOT GO BEYOND THIS NOTICE *(Farne Islands – National Trust)*

PLEASE GO AWAY *(Sign in window of a travel agency)*

BARGAIN BASEMENT UPSTAIRS *(In a London department store)*

WE DISPENSE WITH ACCURACY *(Notice in a Sunderland chemist)*

PLEASE BE SAFE – Do not stand, sit, climb or lean on the zoo's fences. If you fall the animals could eat you and that could make them sick. Thank you. *(Notice in American zoo)*

SLUG PELLETS & AUNT KILLERS FOR SALE

Patrons are requested to remain seated throughout the entire performance. *(Sign in theatre near the public toilets)*

The contents are sufficient for a pie for six persons or twelve small tarts. *(Label on jar of mince)*

Everlasting love, guaranteed to last for five days. *(Label on Valentine bouquets)*

Widows made to order. Send your specifications. *(Ely Standard)*

Need urgent funds. In return will walk around London dressed as a giraffe for a week. *(Camden News)*

Our's are the happiest hour's in town. *(Outside a restaurant at Great Park in Ruberry)*

Crisis as hospital opens with skeleton staff *(Nairobi Times)*

NICKI McKENZIE – Congratulations. You never cease to fail us. Lots of love, Mum, Joe, Ang., Mut. Your are very special: Brad *(Coventry Evening Telegraph)*

UNWANTED Christmas present – Jazz CD (Barry Tyler's original Dixieland Jazz Band) and pair of incontinence pants, both hardly used. *(Royston Crow)*

Owing to circumstances beyond our control the previous list published last week has been changed to the dates given below. We apologise for any incontinence caused. *(Crawley Horticultural Society)*

FREE NEUTERING – Cats Protection is offering to neuter your car for free. *(Newbury Weekly News)*

20 toilet rolls, hardly used, Xmas bargain, £3.50. *(Barrow-in-Furness Evening Mail)*

To touch these wires is instant death. Anyone found doing so will be prosecuted. *(On sign at railway station)*

Do not use orally after using rectally. *(On instructions for electrical thermometer)*

Do not sit under coconut trees. *(On a West Palm beach)*

These rows reserved for parents with children. *(In a church)*

Prescriptions cannot be filled by phone. *(In a clinic)*

Keyboard not present – press any key to continue. *(Error message during boot-up on computer)*

The best of product warnings

Caution: The contents of this bottle should not be fed to fish. *(On a bottle of dog shampoo)*

For external use only *(On a curling iron)*

Warning: This product can burn eyes. *(Also on a curling iron)*

Do not use in the shower. *(On a hair dryer)*

Do not use while sleeping or unconscious. *(On a hand-held massaging device)*

Shin pads cannot protect any part of the body they do not cover. *(On cyclists' shin guards)*

This product not intended for use as a dental drill. *(On an electric rotary tool)*

Do not drive with sunshield in place. *(On a car sunshield)*

Do not use near fire, flame or sparks. *(On an 'Aim-n-Flame' fire lighter)*

Do not eat toner. *(On toner for printer)*

Do not use orally. *(On a toilet-bowl cleaning brush)*

Keep out of children. *(On a butcher's knife)*

Not suitable for children aged 36 months or less. *(On a birthday card for a one-year-old)*

Do not use for drying pets. *(In a microwave manual)*

For use on animals only. *(On an electric cattle prod)*

For use by trained personnel only. *(On a can of air freshener)*

Keep out of reach of children and teenagers. *(Also on a can of air freshener)*

Do not use as earplugs. *(On a pack of silly putty)*

Warning: Has been found to cause cancer in laboratory mice. *(On a box of rat poison)*

Remove infant before folding for storage. *(On a portable walker)*

Do not iron clothes on body. *(On the package for a Rowenta iron)*

For indoor or outdoor use only. *(On the package for Christmas lights)*

Wearing of this garment does not enable you to fly. *(On a child's Superman costume)*

Flies coming into contact with this preparation of DDT die without hope of recovery. *(on the bottle's label)*

Do not use while sleeping. *(On a Sears hairdryer)*

Fits One Head. *(On the box of a hotel-provided shower cap)*

17

Further Education

Students attending Chichester College of Further Education have been advised to sing "God Save The Queen" while frying bacon. Mrs Ivy Davey, their instructress, said: "'God Save The Queen' has a running time of about two minutes – just right for each side of a rasher."

En route to give a lecture in Cleveland, Lancelot Dillger pulled out of his driveway and drove straight into a delivery van. With his car incapacitated, Dillger borrowed his father's, but in hurrying to get to the lecture hall he took a corner too fast and crashed into a truck. Dillger finally arrived to give his lecture, in a taxi. His topic for the evening was "Safe Driving".

Paul Norris's girlfriend could be a very lucky lady. For 20-year-old Dorset Institute of Higher Education banking student Paul has just won £30, and he may spend some of the money on her. *(Bournemouth Evening Echo)*

Students who marry during their course will not be permitted to remain in college. Further, students who are already married must either live with their husbands or make other arrangements with the Dean. *(Syllabus of an Ohio College)*

Britain's 100,000 undergraduates and students returning from vacation this month will be told not to deal with fellow students selling shirts, jewellery and other finery to earn extra cash. But insurance selling at universities and colleges will be allowed because it is considered "enterprising". *(Daily Telegraph)*

Domestic staff in one of Aberdeen University's halls of residence may refuse to work overtime again after a serious incident involving a Brussels sprout last year. *(Gaudie, Aberdeen)*

Three years after she presented a thesis showing that elderly people moved their legs with greater speed when they were in a hurry and reduced the speed of their legs when they were not in a hurry, Miss Stina Fjeleer-Modic, of the Royal University, Stockholm, has submitted a research project on the consumption of cooked meats. Interviewed at her home in Flassturm, Miss Fjeleer-Modic said: "During my investigation I ate 4,756 pork chops in restaurants, canteens, private houses, army barracks, three Institutes for the Insane, and a prison. My study has shown that it is undesirable for a chop to be more than two centimetres thick or to remain in a utensil for more than three minutes after frying."

Some recent PhD theses . . .

The Concept of Social Rage in the Old Testament and the Ancient Near East *(Michigan)*

Homosexual Tendencies in Seagulls *(California)*

Suicide amongst Eskimos in Alaska *(Alaska)*

The Gnome and Its Uses in Certain Old English Poems *(Oxford)*

The Leg Muscles of the Adult Honey Bee *(London)*

The Correct Alignment of Various Fixtures in the Bathroom *(Stockholm)*

Recent Commissions from the government-funded Economic and Social Research Council . . .

Family, friendship and neighbourhood among rural Finns *(1 year: £8,049)*

The development of crying in infancy and its effects on the mother *(3 years: £35,632)*

The social organisation of long-distance traders in Libya *(3 years: £18,962)*

Exchange rates in late mediaeval Europe *(1 year: £5,130)*

Judging the probability of future events *(2 years: £19,686)*

The culture of drinking in an English community *(1 year: £21,040)*

Patients' comprehension of doctors' instructions *(3 years: £11,650)*

Scientists at the University of Pittsburgh researched into how plump women could lose weight after the menopause. It took four years of hard graft, rigorously studying the body fat and cholesterol of 500 volunteers. The conclusion they came to was that a better diet and more exercise would probably do the trick.

According to the National Institute for Healthcare Research in Maryland, when one person hurts another, "forgiveness causes restorations in relationship closeness".

Astonishingly, researchers at the University of Iowa found that youngsters do more exercise if their parents work out in the gym and that they are more likely to smoke if their mothers or fathers smoke.

Professor: Here you see the skull of a chimpanzee – a very rare specimen. There are only two in the country – one is in the National Museum, and I have the other.

Revd William A. Spooner's classic spoonerism telling a student to leave his class for non-attendance and lighting fires:

Sir, you have tasted two whole worms; you have hissed all my mystery lectures and been caught fighting a liar in the quad. You will leave Oxford by the next town drain.

Chelsea College of Physical Education in Eastbourne is recovering with eight broken ribs in a clinic at Sierre in the Rhone Valley. *(Evening Standard)*

One of Princeton University's (USA) best-loved traditions is the Nude Olympics, an event which takes place after the first snowfall. About 350 second-year undergraduates gather at midnight to run naked through the quad, apart from boots and scarves, and emboldened by the demon drink.

CHEATS (INC.) PROSPER: Toronto, 16 December – The old custom of cheating in university essays has become big business in the United States. Last year companies selling essays made about $550,000, and now they are planning to

expand into Canada. One company is training men to manage offices in Toronto, Montreal, and Vancouver, and another is installing a free telephone system for students to order essays from anywhere in North America.

Essays produced under non-examination conditions generally count in North American universities towards a final degree, and education officials say that, if the practice of buying essays is allowed to continue, a college degree will become increasingly less credible as a certification of academic competence.

In the United States last year, the leading essay houses sold more than 10,000 papers. Mr Bill Carmody, who runs the oldest and largest such firm, International Termpapers Incorporated, has built a file of more than 80,000 essays. He has a staff of over four hundred freelance writers who write for a fee of £1 a page. Mr Carmody sells copies for £2 a page. (*Guardian*)

18

Headteachers

It is not easy to be a successful headteacher. Targeted as the "whipping" boys, or girls, of disgruntled staff, governors, Local Education bureaucrats, and OFSTED inspectors, they plough a lonely furrow. Few achieve – though many think they do – majority support within their schools as they attempt to keep as many balls in the air at once, without being kicked in them too frequently. It is only in the period of an OFSTED inspection, when there is unity against the common enemy, and during the relief and euphoria of staff immediately following such a trauma, that the headteacher enjoys temporary respite from belligerent members of the school community.

Is it any wonder then that so many lose concentration and drop howlers, appear miserable, bad tempered or merely insane. The story is told of a particularly depressed head visiting his doctor and being told: "You urgently need a holiday – might I suggest Lourdes?"

Perhaps he's the one who failed to take the advice given, and appeared in a Manchester paper under the heading . . .

DEAD HEAD ON STAFF 25 YEARS

Or maybe he was the one who earned this slot in the Birmingham Post . . .

Tom Brown, 73, a former comprehensive school head-teacher, abandoned his broken-down Skoda on the M5 and took a bus and a train back to his home in Tewkesbury, Gloucestershire – 70 miles away – where, five hours later, police informed him that he had left his 84-year-old wife, Catherine, in the car. Mr Brown said: "I told her not to worry, and set off for the nearest village. I suppose I must have got confused."

And "confused" seems to have been an apt description of the following . . .

At a PTA Annual Meeting, one unfortunate head had the misfortune to utter: "As head of the school I am, of course, the shepherd of the flock. I see our deputy head, Mr Cochrane, as the little crook on the staff." *(Daily Telegraph)*

Headteacher: There is clearly a problem with discipline on the buses . . . Mr White and myself have been disgusting together . . . er . . . discussing . . . sorry about that! *(Parent-teacher meeting)*

The headteacher apologised to the parents because the treacherous winter weather had produced dangerous slippery conditions on the school drive and walkways. Financial constraints had meant that remedial action could not be taken. He informed them that the deputy headteacher responsible for the school budget was gritting his teeth in the circumstances. *(Cleveland school's PTA meeting)*

Mr E. G. Winterton, headmaster, would not comment on the threat. However, he did say: "Some children have been behaving very childishly." *(Doncaster Post)*

Many years ago, Lord Altrincham visited the local grammar school at Chipping Sodbury to present the prizes, and in his introductory speech the head began: "How pleased we are that our Lord has come down today . . ."

And in similar vein . . .

Lord Halifax, the former British ambassador to the United States, once visited a college in Fort Worth, Texas, and addressed the students. The principal introduced him without any problem right up to his closing remark. Then he said: "When the speech is over, if anyone wants to ask questions, the Lord will provide the answers."

The headteacher of a Surrey school once started his assembly with the words: "Today I shall be talking about a 'New Cantament Testicle' – sorry . . . er . . . sorry about that . . . I mean a 'New Testament Canticle'."

The story is told of a headteacher from Buxton who went to pay his condolences to the wife of a retired former colleague who, at an advanced age, had died. As they talked, he put his arm around her shoulders and then supported her twice when her knees buckled. When this happened a third time, the woman looked him in the eye and said: "For God's sake, will you let me kneel down and say a prayer."

The headteacher emerged from his office one morning and announced angrily: "There's just one thing that makes me really mad – bad manners and mathematical incompetence."

A headteacher in Bolton, commenting on the school league

tables in which his school came bottom, with 8% in English and science and 0% in maths, said: "Standards are improving in all four subjects."

Headteacher to staff: There is no point in being pessimistic. It wouldn't work anyway.

Headteacher at prize giving: Once again the Ornithological Society got us off to a flying start.

From "The Teacher" . . .
My sister, a headteacher, lives in a rather remote part of the country and has a breakdown garage next to her house. One morning she answered the phone and heard a voice say: "Can you tell me if there is a Mr Fog there?"

Looking out of her window she saw a man standing at the garage. "Hold on," she said. "There's someone outside. I'll go and ask him his name." With that she dashed outside, asked the man his name and returned to the phone. "Sorry, he isn't Mr Fog," she said.

"Madam," said the voice, "This is the weather centre. We had an agreement with your husband that I would occasionally phone to see what the weather was like in your area. Is there a mist or fog?"

Headmasters can be omnipotent in their little spheres of influence. As Winston Churchill remarked: "Headteachers have powers at their disposal with which prime ministers have never yet been invested."

A headteacher clambered into bed in the middle of winter. "God, your feet are cold," exclaimed his wife. "How many times have I told you," he retorted, "that when we are in bed you can call me 'George'."

Some heads can be pretty miserable, short-tempered or political . . .

My husband and I are shortly to attend an important public dinner, and I understand we shall be seated side by side. He is rather a taciturn man and I feel we shall sit in silence throughout the meal which will look as if we are not on good terms, whereas we are happily married but not in the habit of making conversation to each other. *(Letter in Woman and Home)*

Surrey's County Education Officer is to look into parents' allegations that an infants' school headmaster assaulted a boy with his artificial leg for turning the wrong way in a Maypole dance. *(Times Educational Supplement)*

You haven't been as much an audience as a challenge – and I have to tell you – you won!

. . . of the Association on Alcoholism to speak at the school. He is an excellent speaker and will probably be willing to have a "quick one" with some of us after the evening is over.

The new head was holding his first staff meeting: "I want you all to feel free and speak your mind. I don't want any yes-men around me. I want everybody to give their opinion – even if it does cost you your job."

Note to staff at girls' public school from the headteacher: "Lazy girls should be jogged into action by the news that the Duchess of Kent is doing her own nails."

They say life begins at forty – but so does lumbago, bad eyesight, arthritis, and the habit of telling the same story three times to the same person.

Shortly after his arrival in a new parish, the vicar was asked to conduct the funeral service of a retired headteacher. In the service he announced: "I'm sorry that I cannot pay tribute to the deceased as I did not know him. But if any of you would like to say a few words, please feel free to do so."

There was complete silence. "Now don't be shy," continued the vicar. "I'm sure some of you would like to say a kindly word about your friend." Finally a voice from the back muttered: "His brother was worse."

Some advice for would-be headteachers ...

If you can keep your head while all around are losing theirs, then you clearly don't understand the situation.

Be thankful for your problems, for if they were fewer, someone with less ability would have your job.

If you're not big enough to stand criticism, then you're too small to be praised.

No matter what goes wrong, there is always somebody who knew it would.

Forgive your enemies but never forget their names.

The most knocking is done by those who can't ring the bell.

Speak when you're angry and you'll make the best speech you will ever regret.

A headteacher laughs at his Chair of Governors' jokes not because they are clever, but because *he* is.

Speeches are like babies: Easy to conceive, but hard to deliver.

A meeting is an event at which the minutes are kept and the hours are lost.

A chairman who can smile when things go wrong has found someone to blame it on.

When someone says he is laying all his cards on the table – count them.

A man would do nothing if he waited until he could do it so well that no-one could find fault with it.

The more you say, the less people remember.

Never leave school angry – stay back and fight.

Live every day as if it's your last – and one day, you'll be right.

Always be lenient – sometimes lean one way and sometimes the other.

Rule A: The headteacher is never wrong.
Rule B: If anyone discovers he is wrong, refer to Rule A.

Extracts from heads' speeches . . .

Do you know what it means to go home from school each night to a woman who will give you a little love, a little affection, a little tenderness? To go in and be given a large gin and tonic and then a meal fit for a king? I'll tell you what it means – it means you're in the wrong bloody house! That's what it means.

I'm pleased myself and my wife have found one of the secrets of a long marriage. We take time to go to a nice restaurant or a cosy pub twice a week. A warm corner, subdued lights, soft music, and dancing. She goes on a Tuesday – me on a Friday.

Last year after the inspection we were poised on the edge of a precipice. This year, thank God, we have taken a great leap forward.

Head commenting on burst pipes which flooded some classrooms: "This is the worst disaster since I was appointed."

I will put down my foot with a strong hand.

Father Taylor will now lead us in a few words of silent prayer.

I'm looking for four lads who are quick at picking up music – Right, move that piano over there!

Head to staff: "You are to stand by the fire doors. When I ring the fire alarm, you will allow nobody to leave, explaining it is not a fire – it is just a nuclear attack."

Piece of information from the headteacher of a West Country school at the annual PTA dinner: "As in previous years the evening will conclude with a formal toast to the new president. The champagne will be provided by the retiring president, drunk as usual at midnight."

At another PTA annual dinner, the head's wife was chatting away to the parents on her table about how, as a young girl, before she was married, she was very innocent and naïve. She said: "I didn't even know what a homosexual was until I met my husband."

Headteacher at PTA Annual General Meeting: "Mr Carroll has been elected and has accepted the office of Chairman. We could not get a better man."

Perhaps what heads need for stress is the following, which appeared in a 1920s American chemists' circular . . .

BLANKS NERVE TONIC – drives away nervy symptoms, gives power to brain and body.
LEAVES BEHIND – irritability, indigestion, rheumatism, neuralgia, hysteria, etc.

19

Teachers

The perception the public used to have of the teaching profession as highly respected members of the community has declined rapidly over the years. Changing social outlooks and "mores" have caused their status to plummet and hurtle down the "awe league" along with vicars, priests, doctors and solicitors – to name but a few previously revered occupations. Some of them do little to enhance the profession's reputation . . .

MAN BARKS AT DOG, FINED £5 – Mr Claude Wilson, aged 34, of Benfleet, Essex, a teacher who barked at an Alsatian after it barked at him and had a scuffle with its owner, was fined £5 with £5 costs by Rochford magistrates yesterday. *(The Times)*

Sir, I am a teacher and as such do not like wasting time when I am watching TV. I always like to do something else – at the same time I do foot, finger and eye exercises. I shrug my shoulders and roll my head round and round. During the World Cup, whenever the players took a corner or there was an injury I went down on my back to do a few tummy exercises and circle my legs round in the air. *(Letter in Daily Mail)*

HMI criticized the fact that pupils were not allowed to speak in class. When they wanted to attract the teacher's attention they had to wave a small flag. *(The Times Educational Supplement)*

This is a good teaching film . . . No high or low church bias . . . That is left for the teacher to put in. *(Dawn Trust Films, 1949 catalogue)*

In 1967, Thomas Litz, a teacher in Switzerland, set aside homework, which he marked but forgot to return. It was only in 1988, while sorting through old papers that he came across the exercises. One of the pupils now taught with Thomas at the same school and finally had his work returned after 21 years.

Sometimes what they say can damage their reputations . . .

Whenever I open my mouth, some fool speaks.

This optional subject is compulsory.

Trace events up to Henry VIII.

Draw a Roman soldier you know.

Teacher's instructions on how to use Pritt Stick: "Take off the top and push up the bottom."

Children will not be able to skate on frozen water unless it has been passed by the headteacher.

If you can't keep quiet, shut up!

I want to hear it so quiet that we can hear a mouse dropping.

We must be more tolerant of one another and respect the fact that people have their own opinions, beliefs, likes in music, etc . . . Grigor – get that earring out now!

All right, everybody, line up alphabetically according to height.

Mr Evans, a teacher, claimed the light was green but he was found guilty of failing to obey traffic lights and was fined £100. Mrs Rose Evans told the magistrates the light was blue. She was given an eye test.

My wife, a teacher like myself, left me recently because of my 20-year addiction to gambling. Is there anything that I can do to win her back? *(Letter to the Daily Mail)*

Teachers, however, remain one of the most dedicated of professions and are still prepared to expand their charges' experiences by taking them on trips, which are always stressful . . .

Sir, Last Saturday I took a group of boarders at the prep school where I am housemaster to a football match between Maidenhead United and Ruislip Manor.

On the way to the game the boys were asking me how I chose their Saturday night video. I told them that I took note of the film's classification and tried to avoid bad language, violence and nudity.

We stood behind one of the goals; in the first minute the goalkeeper dropped the ball and uttered an expletive that echoed around the ground.

In the fifth minute, the right winger was scythed to the ground by a vicious tackle that left him writhing in agony. However, I felt pretty sure that my third "video worry" would not occur – then halfway through the second half, a streaker danced across the pitch.

Circular to Exmouth schools . . .

Nine people were bitten by donkeys on Bridlington Sands, 172 were stung by jellyfish and another 13 were bitten by dogs. These are just a few of the 2,186 cases handled by First Aid posts on the town's beaches. Only one casualty required hospital treatment – a male tourist from Holland who had to have a stick of rock removed.

Malcolm Laverty of Bury First School, Pulborough, took his class of ten-year-olds to the coast of North Wales to study a contrasting area of the country. Assembled outside the main gate of Conwy Castle, they were asked to suggest reasons why this particular site was chosen to build such a stronghold. Whilst some eyes glazed over, others surveyed the surrounding area and tried to imagine what it was like hundreds of years ago.

Edward finally raised his hand. "Sir, was it because it could be near the public lavatories?"

Sometimes a visit from a dignitary can be dangerous ...

The Bishop of the Diocese was visiting a Catholic junior school and asked one class of seven-year-olds some questions on religion. He ended up by asking: "Is there anything that God cannot do?" There was silence for a while until one little girl answered: "Please, Sir – Miss says that even God couldn't stop us talking."

But clearly there are some who think teachers are really daft ...

Win a weekend break for two at one of the Care Leisure luxury hotels in the New Forest *or* Take your class on a free visit to one of Central Southern England's leading visitor attractions.

Teachers can be very wise ...

Well done to the Birmingham teacher who, on receiving a letter from her bank manager saying it appeared she was overdrawn, wrote back to ask him to let her know when he was sure. *(Guardian)*

... and dedicated ...

Mr Thomas's teacher colleagues will be sorry to learn that he had an operation last Wednesday and had his leg removed. All being well he should be back on his feet, and back to his job in the classroom, by the end of November. *(Cobar Age, New South Wales)*

We wish him every happiness in his retirement. For over twenty-five years his learning and his wit have enriched the minds of all the boys to whom he taught English. It is true to say that as a teacher he was in a class by himself. *(Sussex school magazine)*

Still, some pupils do show respect . . .

After he had finished robbing her home, the burglar bent over his 81-year-old victim, gave her a kiss, and said: "You were always kind to me." Whereupon the retired Cleveland schoolmistress recognized the intruder as her favourite pupil from 1925, Fergus Wayne. On her positive identification, Fergus was subsequently charged with robbery.

Michael Lee, deputy head of The English Martyrs, Hartlepool, and one-time school team manager, tells the story of preparing his team for their local cup final . . .

We had recently not had a good run, and I decided to give a psychological pep-talk before the match. I told the centre forward to get out there and pretend that he was the best scorer in the North-East. I told the centre half to pretend he was the best defender, and so it continued with each player in the team. The message was positive – pretend you *are* the best. We lost 3-0. I was pacing the changing room, trying to figure out what to say when the big centre forward came in, walked up to me, put his arm around my shoulders and said: "Don't worry, sir – just *pretend* we won."

But what is the reality of teaching beyond the fantasy of what the government's spin doctors would have us believe . . .?

The story is told of the retired woman teacher who died and went up to heaven. St Peter told her that she must spend one day in hell and a second in heaven. Only then could she decide where she wished to stay permanently. She entered the lift and eventually she arrived in hell. It was beautiful – blue skies, wonderful views, golf courses, continental-style streets with umbrellas and wicker chairs. The teacher met some old friends and they had a chat and a "gastronomique" lunch. Afterwards she returned to heaven for her second day, when she spent the time with a couple of angels sitting on a cloud strumming a lyre and singing hymns. When St Peter appeared and asked her what choice she had made, she opted for hell. Down the teacher went on the long journey, and when the door opened she was astonished to see a barren landscape with rubbish everywhere. Her former colleagues were dressed in sackcloth and ashes, picking up garbage and looking totally miserable.

"I don't understand," she said. "What has happened?"

"Ah," Mephistopheles replied. "Yesterday was the interview. Now you're on the staff."

20

Christmas

Christmas, so very special for children, figures prominently in humorous stories of life at school.

The seven toddlers playing the dwarfs in St Joseph's Primary School pantomime in Washington, County Durham, were told to wear their Newcastle United shirts for the part. It was just too much for one of them, who defiantly arrived in his Sunderland top – and, no, he wasn't playing Dopey.

The teacher asked the class of seven-year-olds to name one of the animals in the stable with Jesus when he was born. "A whale, Miss," said George. "Why is that, then, George?" "Well, Miss," came the reply, "we're always singing 'A whale in a manger . . .'"

A seven-year-old boy was told that he was going to be in the Christmas play. A few minutes after he arrived home, the mother of the little lad telephoned the headteacher and said: "Jimmy has just arrived home and he tells me that we have to find a costume for him because he's in the school play and he is going to be a book." The headteacher thought for a moment and said: "No, no . . . he is going to be a page."

"Granny," said the six-year-old returning from school one December evening, "you wouldn't believe it, but we're doing one of those Nativity plays again this Christmas – and it's the same story as last time."

Santa was paying his Christmas visit to St Patrick's junior school and the following conversation took place:
"That's not Santa – that's Mr Joyce, our headteacher," said one little girl.
"No, Lucy. It just looks like Mr Joyce, but it isn't."
Little girl: "Yes it is Miss. Nobody else has got as big a nose as that."

A mother and her eight-year-old son stood in front of Tintoretto's painting of the Nativity. "What I cannot understand," said the boy, "is why Jesus wasn't born in a proper bed when his father was God." His mother explained patiently that Mary and Joseph were on a long journey, that there was no room at the inn and, anyway, they were very poor. "How can they have been very poor when they managed to get themselves painted by a famous painter?"

The teacher had never wanted to use Billy, often a disruptive influence, to entertain the parents in the intermission of the Christmas pantomime. Though he had been desperate to participate, he had been passed over for the more predictably well-behaved John and Sarah. Come the night of the panto, the teacher was obliged to turn to Billy for help when John and Sarah failed to turn up. "Up you get, then, Billy, and do the farmyard impressions you said you were good at." Billy got hold of the mike and confidently began: "Hey you, you little *****, get off that *****ing tractor!"

Overheard in playground . . .

First girl: What can I get Rod for Christmas?
Second girl: Get him a nice book.
First girl: He's already got a book.

SIX MILLION DOLLAR MAN – £3. *(Notice on toy stall at school's Christmas fair)*

When Mary found out from the Angel Gabriel that she was going to be the mother of Jesus, she went off and sang the Magna Carta.

And they brought gifts of Gold, Frankenstein and Myrrh.

During the Christmas processional hymn, the heel of a girl chorister caught in a grating. Not wishing to hold up the ceremony, she marched on minus a shoe. Moved to chivalry, a male chorister following tried to pick up the shoe. Unfortunately the heel was stuck firmly in the grating, so again not wanting to hold up the procession, the chorister picked up the whole lot and continued up the nave. The officiating clergyman promptly fell into the hole. *(Ely Diocesan newsletter)*

GO MAD THIS WEEKEND – BUY SOME BEEF.

(Sign at restaurant where a North Yorkshire school staff held their festive meal)

And have you ever wondered where some of the children's toys end up . . .?

"Youngsters think the toilet is a safe hiding place," said Derek Waites, a manager at Northumbrian Water's Stockton-on-Tees treatment works. "At Christmas we can

tell what the most popular presents were. Toys float through miles of sewers to our works. We've fished out quite a number of Action Men. We have even found a 12ft python. It gave one of our men a shock – he had gone to investigate a blockage and it landed on his head. Fortunately it was dead. False teeth are also found in sewage works at this time of year. Some people have too much to drink and lose them. One man rang up to ask if we had found them. He tried on a set we had fished out, but when he put them in, they weren't his."

Help can come in the most unusual of ways at Christmas . . .

Eric: My wife said the other day that I'd done absolutely nothing to help with the Christmas dinner. Absolutely nothing.
Ernie: What did you say?
Eric: I said, "What! Look at the turkey – I bought it, I've plucked it and I've stuffed it!"
Ernie: Good for you!
Eric: Now all she's got to do is kill it and put it in the oven.

21

Names

Sometimes the appropriate name appears to have been designed for the circumstances . . .

12.00 IT'S IN THE CLOSET,
IT'S UNDER THE BED. A
documentary about
vampires, werewolves,
and other such favourite
screen creepies.
12.25 NIGHT THOUGHTS
with the Revd Kenneth
Wolfe. Close
(Guardian)

He said both of the student's assailants were white, aged about 22, and one had a large "buzzard-like" nose. Witnesses should contact Mr Bird of Hornchurch CID. *(Romford Recorder)*

Adult education students at Brentwood, Essex, are taught woodwork by Mr Joiner, art by Mr Painter, seamanship by Mr Waterman and flower arranging by Miss Baskett. Belly dancing is taught by Miss Button.

The New Scientist has drawn scholars' attention to the *The British Journal of Urology*, by J. Splatt and D. Weedon; and also to the fact that there is W.I. Ball, an eye surgeon, and J. Lust, a New Zealand sex therapist.

Entry in the DEATHS column of the *Veterinary Record* . . . Dr P. J. Posthumus RGM writes – "Dr Peter Jacobus Posthumus, who died in August 1991, . . ."

Some people are given names they would never have chosen for themselves. A perusal of school registers from any large comprehensive school will reveal at least a couple of unusual names, and here are a few examples from County Durham . . .

Teresa Green, C. Lion, Brad Hall, R. Soul, Brian Olivers *(initials)*, Annette Kirton, Duncan Biscuit, Orson Carte, Sean A. Legg, Russell Sprout, A. Pratt, Walter Wall, Rose Berry, Eileen Dover.

The great-great-grandson of Carlos III of Spain, Don Alfonso de Borbon y Borbon (1866-1934), had 94 first names.

My Father, Albert Hall, was born in 1883 and ran away from home as a young boy. Asked his name by the recruiting sergeant, he said: 'Hall, Sir.' 'First name?' 'Er . . . Albert, Sir.' To which the sergeant replied: 'Now, you fellow, none of your clever stuff here.'"

The longest name appearing on a birth certificate is that of **Rhoshandiatellyneshiaunneveshenk**, of Beaumont, Texas.

Chris Freddi's *Book of Funny Names* includes a number of referees with unusual names for their chosen occupation:

Charlie Faultless, a Scottish referee from the 1950s, and Segar Richard B****** from the 1880s.

In 1997, GB Information compiled a list of the unfortunate, but genuine, names of individuals who must find the Christmas period particularly trying . . .

•17 Mary Christmases •4 Holly Berrys •2 J Christs •Sandra Claus, who lives in Yorkshire •3 Kings from Leyton Orient •2 Turkeys from London •5 Terry Tubbys from Birmingham •73 people in Britain called La La and 262 named Po, Dipsy and Tinky.

Why is it that in the world of entertainment, and especially among the musical fraternity, there is a penchant for "different" names? It must be hard enough to have to carry the burden of a successful parent without having to be additionally burdened with an outrageous name. Of the nine parents listed below, it is noticeable that all but one – Woody Allen – possesses a regular Christian name. Americans do appear to have an inclination for bestowing the most bizarre names on their offspring. One would have thought that, had these parents been serious in their choice of names for their children, they might, at least, have changed their own to reflect their madness . . .

Dandelion *(daughter of Keith Richards)*
Free *(son of Barbara Hershey)*
Satchel *(son of Woody Allen)*
Moon Unit *(daughter of Frank Zappa)*
Dweezil *(son of Frank Zappa)*
Rain *(daughter of Richard Pryor)*
Zowie *(son of David Bowie)*
Sage Moonbled *(son of Sylvester Stallone)*
God *(daughter of Grace Slick)*

Others are just not satisfied with the name they have been given . . .

The case was that of William David Coleman, aged 22 of Liverpool, who denied being in unlawful possession of a motor car, a suitcase, and a guitar, and obtaining a driving licence by giving a false name of William Peter Johaan Karl Amsberg von Hapsburg Schleswig Holenstein von Hanover Zu Amsterdam. *(Liverpool Echo)*

In the United States the determination to derive commercial or other benefit from being the last listing in the local telephone directory has resulted in self-given names starting with up to 9 "Z"s – an extreme example being "Zachary Zzzzzzzzzra" in the San Francisco book.

And coming together can be such fun . . .

BONE-MARROW: The engagement is announced between Joanne Louise, only daughter of Mr and Mrs D. Marrow, and Kevin James Bone, only son of Mr and Mrs J. Bone. *(Bury Times)*

Dr I.L.C. Sly and Miss N.J.E. Fox: The engagement is announced between Ian, younger son of the late Capt L.T. Sly and of Mrs A.G. Sly, of Canterbury, Kent, and Nikola, only daughter of Mr and Mrs N.E. Fox, of Great Bealings, Suffolk. *(Press and Journal)*

COLMAN-BALLS: The engagement is announced between TIMOTHY, son of Mr and Mrs B.P. Colman, of Fakenham Road, Drayton, and MARIE, daughter of Mr and Mrs R.E. Balls, of West End, Old Costessey. Love from both families. *(Eastern Evening News)*

And a different type of coming together . . .

The new teacher was going around the class asking names.
"And what is *your* name?" he asked the little lad.
"Alex," came the reply.
"Alex what?" asked the teacher.
". . .-ander," was the response.

Then some people make a right mess of it . . .

"Now, Muhammad, that's a popular Christian name, isn't it?" *(Interviewer of Muhammad Ali, 1980)*

The proud mother was so delighted with the way the doctor had eased her through her delivery she said she would like to name the boy after him. "What's your name, doctor?" she asked. "Clarence," he replied. For a moment the young mother was thoughtful, and then she said: "You don't have a middle name, do you?"

22

Would You Believe It?

AUSTIN ALLEGRO 1300. Taxed, MoT, radio. £395 ono. Btn. 776155 after 6pm.
AUSTIN-Cyril. Forever in our thoughts. Ivy, Jim & family.
AUSTIN PRINCESS 2000 HL, 1979, Superb, low mileage, history. £10,956. 673620. *(London Evening Standard small ads)*

Spelling tests in English and French are to be demanded in Parliament for officials responsible for British passports. The current passport contains a non-existent French word and the visitor's passport misspells '"Gibraltar". When an MP queried it with the Passport Office, he was told: "Oh, really, have we? We spelt Sweden wrong in the last issue." *(Daily Telegraph)*

Can anyone recommend school for boy 14, where reincarnation is accepted and astrology understood? *(Advert in Daily Telegraph)*

Court Report from *Reynolds News* . . .

Mr T. Belk, clerk to the Middlesbrough magistrates: Why have you not sent your child to school regularly?
Mr J. T. Howlett: Because he has no boots.

Clerk: But you went to school without boots when you were young, did you not?
Parent: Yes, sir.
Clerk: Then why cannot your son do the same? It will not do him any harm.

Brighton Film Studios are making a Conservative propaganda film without a name. The public will not be allowed to see it. *(Brighton and Hove Gazette)*

How many of us at school realised that Perkin Warbeck was a figure in the Jewish World plot against Aryan sovereignty? *(Aristocracy, published by the Imperial Fascist League)*

Newport Council are holding an open day at their Telford Depot in Corporation Road on Wednesday 1 July. Among the attractions is a sewer jetting model display, a display of cesspit emptying plant and graffiti removal techniques. *(Newport Free Press)*

Renewal notices for three books from Lincoln City Library have come from the Saudi Arabian desert, where Mr Ronald Paing, a local schoolteacher, inadvertently took them on a nine months' stay in Mubbaraz. The books were treatises on central heating. *(Guardian)*

And now, just before *The Sinking of the Scharnhost*, attention all shipping. *(BBC Radio 4 continuity, 1984)*

The road leading to St Michael's School has been affected by severe flooding – traffic is reduced to a crawl. *(BBC Radio 2 traffic news, 1984)*

We are now going over to our reporter who accompanied the teachers' march on one leg. *(BBC News, 1981)*

There will be widespread fist and mog. *(Radio 4)*

More about that delay on British Rail Southern Region. We have our reporter on the line . . . *(Radio 4)*

Defending solicitor, Mr Richard Snow, suggested that Brother Finbarr, a teacher, was mistaken in identifying his client, as he had spoken to him through a row of runner beans. *(M. Rendall, Western Gazette)*

£12,000 worth of compact discs were stolen from Morecambe Library while a crime prevention exhibition was taking place in an adjoining room.

If all the pupils who fell asleep during assemblies were laid end to end, they would be much more comfortable.

There was the dyslexic ex-pupil who held up a bank with a gnu.

The school chaplain told the governors that an increased number of pupils were attending services and also reported that death watch beetle had been confirmed in the chapel.

Smoke alarm firm, CIG-arrête, has produced a vandal-proof alarm to be installed in school toilets to catch rule breakers. "This should *weed* out the offenders and gradually *filter* out the habit," says a spokesman.

A teacher in Thornaby village primary school, Cleveland, confiscated a white powder being passed around in tinfoil by an 11-year-old boy. A crime lab identified the powder as amphetamine sulphate (Speed or Whizz); the boy was interviewed by Cleveland police and suspended from school for 15 days. Five weeks later, the police admitted that "detailed analysis" showed the powder was sherbet, as the boy had insisted from the start.

When Middlesbrough Football Club were relegated at the end of the '96-'97 season from the Premiership, fifth formers at the prestigious St Michael's RC School in Billingham held what they described quite inadvertently as their "Going Down" dance at the team's Cellnet Stadium.

When newscaster Trevor McDonald launched his campaign to improve spoken English, he was interviewed on Radio 4. "What are you hoping to achieve?" asked Sue McGregor. "Well, Sue," responded Trevor. "The things I'm hoping to achieve is . . ." Ah, well.

IT'S RUBBER-LEGS ROBERTS. Did you go to school with

Peter "Rubber-Legs" Roberts who, at the age of 15 in 1953, was a pupil at Rossington Secondary Modern School? Can anyone remember bullying Peter at school? If so, he would like to invite you to spend a weekend on his yacht in Cannes, and to discuss your problem. Peter bears no ill will to any of his school chums, sends them his best wishes for 1999, and hopes they are all keeping well. He also hopes his old school pals will reply to his letter through the *Villager*. *(From Doncaster's Villager, January 1999)*

23

Inspectors

OFSTED inspectors are one group of bureaucrats who are not highly regarded within the ranks of teachers. They tend to be seen as the instruments of ivory-towered mandarins who are detached from the real world of education. There exists a yawning gap of credibility between those who inspect and those who teach – a situation which has been described as "similar to surviving life as a foot-soldier in the trenches, where the strategists ten miles from the front have an unrealistic grand plan to win the war".

Hence the reason why sarcastic and contemptuous cracks and quips, examples of which follow, are circulating throughout staffrooms as teachers wreak secret revenge on these agents of depression and torture, the traffic wardens of the education world.

The judge addressed the witness in the box. "Now," said the judge, "you do understand that you have sworn to tell the truth, the whole truth and nothing but the truth?"

"Well," the witness replied, "I think I ought to tell you that by profession I am an OFSTED inspector."

Tony Blair in Cabinet: "There seem to be only two possible ways of solving this fiasco and constant changing in education. There is the miraculous and the practical. We can all kneel down and pray that God will intervene and solve the problems. That's the practical. The miraculous is that you, David *[Blunkett]*, and OFSTED sit down and discuss it sensibly with the teachers.

Question: What is the difference between a Rottweiler and an OFSTED inspector?

Answers ...
You can have a Rottweiler put down.
A Rottweiler has only one face.
A Rottweiler doesn't smile just before it attacks.
A Rottweiler is less aggressive.

And others ...
Q: How is an OFSTED inspector like a bank robber?
A: Once he's done the job he gets away as fast as he can.

Q: Why is an OFSTED inspector like a eunuch?
A: A eunuch knows what to do but cannot do it himself.

Q: What's the difference between a terrorist and an OFSTED inspector?
A: You can negotiate with a terrorist.

Q: What do you call a group of failed teachers?
A: An OFSTED team.

Q: Why is an OFSTED inspection like childbirth?
A: It takes months of preparation, is over in a short time, but the effects can last for life.

Q: What's the difference between an OFSTED inspector and a haddock?
A: One's wet and slippery and the other is a fish.

Q: How many OFSTED inspectors does it take to change a light bulb?
A: Ten. One to remove the bulb and the other nine to decide whether it should be replaced or put under special measures.
Alternative answer: One. The lay inspector is an electrician.

OR . . .

How about six?

1 to change it
1 to read the plan on how to change it
1 to observe the changing
1 to write it up
1 to assess
and 1 who we are never quite sure why they are there, but it makes for an even number.

OR . . .

We are unable to give you that information until the report is published.

There's only one f-in OFSTED
But that's quite enough for us.
But with no f-in lesson plans
There's one hell of an f-in fuss.

We tried to treat the lead inspector as a treasure – bury him with care and affection.

Q: Why are OFSTED inspectors like pigeons?
A: They should never be looked up to.

You can tell an OFSTED inspector, but you can't tell him much.

Q: How do OFSTED inspectors keep fit?
A: They jump to conclusions.

OFSTED inspector: Everybody hates me.
Wife: Don't be silly. Everybody hasn't met you yet.

Seven-year-old to visiting OFSTED Inspector: Our teacher has been very busy lately. He's marked all our books, which he never does, and he's put some pictures up on the walls.

The inspector was talking to a little girl, who informed him that she had heard her teacher talking to the headteacher, and she was so pleased the inspector had come. "Miss said your turning up today was all she needed."

The greatest number of schools attended by a pupil is 265, by American Wilma Williams from 1933-1943, when her parents were in show business.

The inspector was in a class of eight-year-olds in York. Robert was listening attentively as his teacher described Paris. "A beautiful city," she enthused, "with elegant buildings and fine old churches, art and pavement cafés. A romantic city. Have any of you ever been to Paris?" Robert had. "Robert, you lucky boy. When did you go? Last summer? With your parents? Oh, you lucky boy. Did you like it?" "Not really," said Robert. "It was full of dog s**t."

David Blunkett's faith in his saintly Chief Schools' Inspector appears to be shared by the Muslim Education

Co-ordinating Council, which advertised a speech by "Mr Christ Woodhead" at its forthcoming conference. *(Mail On Sunday)*

24

Administration

Sometimes one wonders whether those who have such an impact upon education – politicians, education officials and governors – read what they have written, or think before opening their mouths.

The following examples would seem to give some credence to this observation of Carl C. Byers: "An Education Committee – a group of the unfit appointed by the unwilling to do the unnecessary."

My purpose in writing to you is to notify you of the anticipated changes for the 1993/4 survey. To date there are no major changes expected, but should any occur we will write and let you know. *(Letter to all Chief Education Officers from Department for Education statistician)*

In the latest issue of *Professional Administration*, the official publication of the Institute of Chartered Secretaries and Administrators, the first article is headed: "Great educational expenditure has not produced the long-awaited economic expansion." It is signed by C. A. Horn, PhD, MSc, BSc (Econ), LLB MBIM, FCIS, FIWSP.

Labour councillors believe that including formal academic

qualifications in job advertisements leads to discrimination against people who done badly at school. *(Reading Chronicle)*

Sir Douglas denied that the relatively high level of public school and Oxbridge-educated people selected for high Civil Service grades was the result of any deliberate bias. There was a danger that the Civil Service might appear to be "perpetuating itself in its own image", but one explanation could be that talents were inherited and talented parents were wealthy enough to send their children to public schools. *(Guardian)*

After my marriage I taught a class of backward children in a county primary school. I feel I have the right kind of training and experience to understand your problems and represent you on the City Council. *(From an election address)*

The governing body vetoed the idea of extra litter bins being placed in the school ground because, they said, they would just attract more rubbish.

Safety experts say school bus passengers should be belted.

On Cleveland Radio there was a report about educational spending cuts in North Yorkshire. A spokesman stated: "As a result of cuts, the library project at Easingwold School will have to be shelved."

Mr Chairman, I move that all fire extinguishers be examined ten days before every fire. *(School governors' meeting)*

"I am not against comprehensive education but I want it within the grammar school framework," Councillor Stirrup explained.

"Women already hold too many of the best posts," declared Councillor W.H.S. Colbourn at yesterday's meeting of the Gloucester Education Committee. Councillor Colbourn said that if women were to be given all the best jobs men would soon be pushed out altogether and in a few generations human life would become extinct. *(Daily Herald)*

"The school is next to a graveyard, so what is wrong with building a funeral parlour?" Thus said Councillor Edwards: "Let's breathe a bit of life into the place." *(Hoylake and West Kirby News)*

The Mayor said he was a great animal lover, and he detested people who were cruel to animals. "It is bad enough with children, but when it comes to dumb animals it is terrible." *(Dorset County Chronicle)*

Council bosses have ordered teachers at a Derbyshire school to move a children's Wendy House because it doesn't have planning permission.

He urged that a pedestrian crossing should be installed. He knew the boys would not use the crossing, but if they put one there, then the Council's responsibility would end. *(Evening Standard)*

Mr Chairman, I have to tell you that I think this proposal to merge the two schools is completely phony with a capital F.

A councillor remarked at a teacher's interview that he had noticed from his application the candidate had attended a Physical Education College – when he had written "FE College".

Minister of Sport, Denis Howell, thinks we should start preparing for retirement from an early age. "It's as important as planning for a career," he claims. He says: "I believe we should start preparing people for retirement while they are still at secondary school, though people look at me as though I am mad when I say that." *(Evening Standard)*

Additionally, there is little doubt that, outside the core, the curricular guidelines will be far less specific, with the exception, perhaps, of technology, and Mr Baker's pet, history. But one can hardly expect sensitivity from a man who reads *The Charge of the Light Brigade* to a class of Russian children.

Others are merely thoughtless . . .

Mrs Jessie Kitchen, aged 71, of Dennis Close, Ashford, Middlesex, was given a canteen of cutlery by her employers, Surrey County Council, for 30 years' service [in school meals] – followed by a bill for £1.12 as part payment for the gift. The Council said her choice cost just over the £25 limit for 30 years' service, and she had to be charged the extra. *(Guardian)*

"I must admit that it was an awful moment," said Councillor Cherry Westburn, Chairwoman of the Raymeadow Education Committee. No sooner had Councillor Anthony Clarke finished reading his report on current teaching methods than Councillor Grey began to attack him, saying that his views were expensive and old-fashioned. In the middle of all this, Councillor Clarke went white and buried his face in his hands, whereupon Councillor Grey shouted: "I hope you are burying your head in shame!" But in fact Councillor Clarke was dying of a heart attack.

The full cost of the government-subsidised school dinner is about 49p, made up of 16p for food and 33p for administration. *(Daily Telegraph)*

GREAT SERVICE TO EDUCATION ...
Mr Eric Jones resigns from
County Committees *(Salisbury Journal)*

25

Some Strange Translations At Home And Abroad

Sometimes the use of inappropriate English translations for various products and instructions results in some bizarre offerings:

French Creeps *(Crepes)*

Garlic Coffee *(Gaelic)*

Indonesian Nazi Goreng

Muscles of Marines

Lobster Thermos

Pork with fresh garbage *(cabbage)*

Prawn cock and tail

Roasted Duck let loose *(Free Range Duck)*

French fried ships *(chips)*

Strawberry Crap

Fresh caut soul

Sweat from the trolley

Teppan Yaki – Before your cooked right eyes

Toes with butter and jam

Hen Soop Soap of the day

Melon and prostitute hams

Eyes cream

Coffee Eggspress

Little Kids – Roasted or at spit

Lemon jews

Irish Stew a L'Ecossaise

Cock in wine/Lioness cutlet *(Coq au vin/Lyonnaise cutlet)*

Dreaded veal cutlet with potatoes in cream *(Breaded . . .)*

This week's speciality – MULES MARINERE

Our wines leave you nothing to hope for *(Switzerland Hotel)*

When translated into Chinese, the Kentucky Fried Chicken slogan 'finger-lickin' good' came out as 'eat your fingers off'.

Outside a Hong Kong tailor's shop: 'Ladies may have a fit upstairs'.

Colgate introduced a toothpaste in France called 'Cue', the name of a notorious pornographic magazine.

The genuine antics in your room come from our family castle. *(In a Bed & Breakfast in France)*

Special cocktails for the ladies with nuts. *(In a Tokyo bar)*

Please to bathe inside the tub. *(In a Japanese hotel room)*

Stop – Drive Sideways. *(Diversion sign in Kyushi, Japan)*

Take one of our horse-driven city tours – we guarantee no miscarriages. *(In a Czechoslovakian tourist agency)*

In an effort to boost orange juice sales in England, a campaign was devised to extol the drink's eye-opening, pick-me-up qualities. Hence the slogan, 'Orange juice. It gets your pecker up'.

Visitors are expected to complain at the office between the hours of 9 and 11 a.m. daily. *(In a hotel in Athens)*

Salad a firm's own make; limpid red beet soup with cheesy dumplings in the form of a finger; roasted duck let loose; beef rashers beaten up in the country people's fashion. *(From a Polish hotel menu)*

Ford had a problem in Brazil when the Pinto flopped. The company found out that Pinto was Brazilian slang for 'tiny male genitals'. Ford pried all the nameplates off and substituted Corcel, which means horse.

Taiwan – the translation of the Pepsi slogan 'Come alive with the Pepsi Generation' came out as 'Pepsi will bring your ancestors back from the dead'.

Yugoslavia – in the Europa Hotel, in Sarajevo, you will find this message on every door: 'Guests should announce the abandonment of theirs rooms before 12 o'clock, emptying the room at the latest until 14 o'clock, for the use of the room before 5 at the arrival or after the 16 o'clock at the departure, will be billed as one night more.'

The lift is being fixed for the next day. During that time we regret that you will be unbearable. *(Bucharest)*

The flattening of underwear with pleasure is the job of the chambermaid. *(Yugoslavia)*

You are invited to take advantage of the chambermaid. *(Japan)*

You are invited to visit the cemetery where famous Russians are buried daily. *(Russia)*

Not to perambulate the corridors in the hours of repose in the boots of ascension. *(Austria)*

Drop your trousers here for best results. *(Bangkok cleaners)*

Dresses for street walking. *(Paris dress shop)*

Because of the impropriety of entertaining guests of the opposite sex in the bedroom, it is suggested that the lobby be used for this purpose. *(Zurich)*

Teeth extracted by the latest Methodists. *(Hong Kong dentist)*

Ladies, leave your clothes here and spend the afternoon having a good time. *(Rome laundry)*

It is forbidden to enter a woman even a foreigner dressed as a man. *(Bangkok Temple)*

We take your bags and send them in all directions. *(Copenhagen Airport)*

If this is your first visit to the USSR, you are welcome to it. *(in a Moscow hotel)*

Our nylons cost more than common, but you'll find they are best in the long run. *(Tokyo shop)*

Customers giving orders will be promptly executed. *(Notice in Bombay tailor's)*

Haircutting while you wait. *(Dublin Barber's)*

Please do not lock the door as we have lost the key. *(St David's School)*

The best place in town to take a leak. *(Outside a radiator repair shop)*

We are closed on Labour Day. *(Outside a maternity clothes shop)*

To stop the drip, turn cock to the right. *(In a Finnish washroom)*

No children allowed. *(In a Florida maternity ward)*

No trespassing. Violators will be prosecuted – Sisters of Mercy. *(On a gate outside a convent)*

La orquesta ejecuto el 'Good sabe the Queen', *coreado por la concurencia, lo mismo que el* 'Forisa Folley good fillow'. *(La Nacion, Buenos Aires)*

Push Push. *(On the door of a maternity hospital)*

Closed due to illness. *(In a health shop window)*

Please knock loudly – bell out of order. *(On electrical repair shop door)*

Don't sleep with a drip – call your plumber. *(On a plumber's van)*

Closing down – thanks to all our customers. *(Outside a shop)*

Do not leave this restaurant without sampling the tart of this house. *(Swiss restaurant)*

Our curries are so delicious you will repeat often. *(Manchester restaurant)*

CHICKEN TIKKA ....
£2.00
Homeless chicken marinated in yoghurt and spices then baked
(Megna takeaway menu, Narbeth)

But sometimes it isn't easy to make yourself understood, even in England.

The appetising smell of chips drew us to a Chinese restaurant at Penrith. We hadn't much time so I asked an immaculate waiter if we could 'carry out'. He looked puzzled. I tried again, speaking very slowly. Did they have 'carry-outs'? 'Ah,' he said, brightening, 'We have chicken curry rice. But we do not have curry oot.' We laughed all the rest of the way to Blackpool. *(The Sunday Post)*